UNDESIRABLE

MM BEAR/WOLF SHIFTER DARK ROMANCE

JT FADER

STEAMBATH PRESS

Published by Steambath Press

A Creekside Valley Dark Romance

Cover art by Leigh Jarrett

eBook Edition published: December 2025

ISBN: 978-1-998008-98-8

CONTENTS

AUTHOR'S NOTES

This story is a **dark** romance with a happy ending. It contains glimpses into the world of drug and alcohol addiction, homelessness, sex work, including pseudo-sexual assault, cults, gay conversion therapy, physical abuse, and gay pornography work.

If these themes might be triggering for you, please approach this book with caution.

Chapter 1

LUCAS

My head was pounding so hard, I thought the throbbing pain was going to force my eyeballs out of their sockets. Even my damned jaw hurt. My brother Maddox's stag night had been intense.

I pulled my pillow over my eyes to keep the light streaming in through my Metro City hotel room window from contributing to the daggers already piercing my brain.

I couldn't settle back to sleep.

Through the epic hangover fog, I detected a scent.

Alpha.

Bear.

I rolled my sore eyes.

Great.

I'd brought someone back to my hotel room for a quick drunken romp. I didn't remember anything about it, but there was someone in bed with me. I could hear him breathing.

I wrinkled my nose.

He smelled vaguely familiar.

I'd probably gotten a massive scent infusion off him while I fucked him.

I thanked the goddesses of the stars; he wasn't an Omega wolf in heat. The last thing I needed was a pup running around while I adjusted to my new pack responsibilities.

Maddox had found love in Metro City, and he'd handed over the reins of pack leader of the East Creekside wolf pack to me. We'd spent months going over everything.

The sudden addition of a mate and pup would complicate things, but I would roll with the scenario if it happened, because it was the right thing to do. If I got an Omega wolf pregnant, I would offer to become their mate if they wanted me—female or male. I was into both sexes.

The bear shifter behind me was most definitely male.

A bear.

Really, Lucas?

I let out a long sigh, which made him stir.

He groaned and muttered, "Fuck."

That was my cue to get out of bed and hit the bathroom. Maybe when I came back, he would be gone. I looked over my shoulder at him as I plodded across the room, nauseous as hell.

My lover for the night had the blankets pulled over his head.

He must be suffering as badly as I was.

In the bathroom, I had to support myself against the wall as I relieved my poor bladder. I hazily remembered fucking my guest in a few different positions before crashing on the bed.

I flushed the toilet.

Memories were drifting in. He'd been experienced and fun.

I stepped out of the bathroom, gasped, and nearly stumbled and dropped onto my knees. Sitting up in bed looking freshly fucked, hungover, and surprisingly handsome all at once ....

Jesse

I shook my head as I walked to the foot of the bed. "Please tell me I'm imagining things."

Jesse laughed. "Um ... wow ... Lucas ... okay."

"Stop laughing. It's not funny."

"Kind of is." Jesse folded the edge of the sheet over the blanket, showing off his abs.

Hairy and beyond fucking lickable.

Suddenly, I was very aware that I was nude in front of Rory and Carter's friend, and he was causing my cock to thicken. I went in search of my clothes that were strewn about on the floor.

"Want to go again?" Jesse asked and lowered the sheet further, exposing his firm dick.

I stared at him, incredulous. "No. I do *not* want to *go* again."

"Pretty sure we had fun."

"Maybe, but this shouldn't have happened." After dressing, I glanced around and caught sight of something on the bedside table on my side of the bed—a gold-colored ring.

I didn't own a ring.

Jesse saw where I was looking and raised his left hand.

A ring identical to the one I'd spotted on the table was on his ring finger.

Oh, hell no.

My heart rate went into overdrive, bringing me to the verge of outright panic.

What the hell happened last night?

"Please tell me we didn't ...," I whispered.

Jesse's brow furrowed. "I don't remember ... but it looks like we did."

The technicalities of the epic nightmare unfolding stormed my brain. Cross-species couldn't marry, but if we'd gone to a human chapel, they wouldn't have known we were shifters.

"Do you remember *anything*?" I asked.

"I remember bumping into you at Club Noir."

I searched my memory. The stag party had gone out dancing after drinking way too much in Maddox's hotel room. Didn't help that I was lightweight. It was rare that I touched alcohol.

I looked at Jesse.

This was a perfect reason why I didn't.

I remembered talking to him by the bar, then moving to a table for some privacy. We'd had lots to talk about, but I couldn't remember what. I covered my forehand with my hand.

Emerging in my mind, a memory of kissing Jesse in the back of a taxi.

The kiss had been hot.

So hot.

Surely, we had nothing in common. But maybe that's what had fascinated me about him. I knew his history with addiction and homelessness. Carter had revealed some of their lives together on the streets to me over time. The drugs, alcohol, and his love relationship with Jesse.

I went over to the ring on the table, lifted it, and set it in my palm.

"We need to get this annulled or something," I said.

"Do we?"

I glared at him. "Don't fuck around, Jesse. You are *not* my mate."

Jesse chuckled.

Not sure what he was finding so fucking funny.

"You should see your face," he said. "The revulsion and panic are next level."

I tried to adjust my expression.

Obviously, the negatives hadn't been there last night. Jesse wasn't even my type. For one, he was an Alpha, and a small one at that. Pretty sure I tossed him around a fair bit last night. For another, he was a bear, which typically didn't stop me from physical encounters.

But this was Jesse.

Sure, he was sexy as fuck, but he was *not* someone I wanted in my life. He was a trainwreck. Carter hadn't said as much aloud, but he voiced his daily woes at work, including going to Jesse's three times a week to check on him. The bear was not partner *or* even friend material.

Jessie was a junkie, and I was somehow married to him now.

No one could ever find out about this.

I picked up and tossed his clothes at him. "You need to go."

Jesse swung his legs out of bed. "You're no fun." When he stood, I took a step back. He was gorgeous. Long, lean muscles capped off by abundant, groomed facial hair that suited him.

I remembered the feel of it on my chin and lips.

And dammit ... on my ass, too.

I thought about spiders crawling all over me to suppress the excitement of my cock. But Jesse had a good nose. He looked at my eyes, then my crotch, and back again, and smiled.

My arousal had been noted.

I fixed my gaze on his. His eyes were the color of a tropical ocean, so blue that it would be easy to drown in them. I had images of staring down into them, enthralled as I fucked him.

There was a remnant of what I had felt in the early hours with him, a longing for him—a connection despite our differences. Of all the crazy things, I'd felt love for him.

Had I told him I loved him?

Oh, my god, I did.

We must have dashed out some time after that to find a 24-hour chapel.

I scrubbed my hands up and down my face to clear the gathering images in my mind. A tacky white chapel. An arch covered in fake pink roses. A man wearing a worn, white tuxedo.

Gold rings out of a tattered box of many such rings.

"Are you okay?" Jesse asked. "It's not a big deal. We had a wild night together. That's it."

I clung to the hair above my forehead, my mind whirring. "I need to talk to my lawyer."

"Sure, whatever." Jesse tucked a white pill into his mouth, swallowed it dry, pulled on his clothes, stealing my view of his incredible body, and headed for the door, a satchel in hand. "You know where to find me when you get it sorted. If I'm not home, get Carter to track me down."

Then he was gone, and I sank onto the edge of the bed.

The sex had been amazing. Glimpses of memories told me that much. Jesse had been an adventurous and responsive lover. I shook my head and groaned—reminding myself who he was.

Dammit.

Jesse was the best I'd ever been with.

I wanted more.

Chapter 2

JESSE

I was running behind, but they'd wait for me. I was doing a gang-bang scene today, and they needed my special skills to deliver what the viewers wanted. Cocks, ass, and copious cum.

I'd been with St. Sebastian Studios for almost six months, working most weekends, and I was earning $500/scene now because I had no hard limits—vanilla sex to nasty degradation.

I was all over it.

I typed in the code, pulled open the opaque studio door, and jogged up the stairs to the chilly reception area. They kept the heat to a minimum to save money, and so we wouldn't look sweaty unless that's what they wanted. Then the heat lamps would come on, making us glisten.

My ass was certainly warmed up for my scene. I'm not sure how many times Lucas and I fucked last night, but it was significant. A bubbly, blond, twink receptionist greeted me.

"Good morning, Jet."

Jet was my stage name. Not too different from my real name, so I wouldn't get confused if I were floating on too many drugs. I usually only did poppers if they'd let me, and cocaine.

Jesse Carter was relegated to a high shelf for the next few hours.

I smiled at the beautiful, young human male. "Am I in trouble yet?"

"There's some grumbling happening. You'd better hurry."

I picked up the pace as I walked the hallway to the dressing room. Inside were three models with whom I had done scenes. They were an amiable bunch. I considered them to be friends.

"Hey, Jet, you are *so* late," Sunny, yet another blond twink, said. "Michael is freaking out." Sunny was practically bouncing on his heels, his exuberant personality impossible to contain.

"I had a busy night," I replied. "Took me a while to get going."

Baron, a tall, robust, but gentle giant, who had topped me many times, looked at me, and his gaze landed on my ring finger. "I'll say. Who's the lucky guy?"

"No one." I slipped the ring off my finger and stuffed it into my jeans' pocket. "Well, not *no one*. I hooked up with my best friend's boss last night. It was a blur that resulted in marriage."

"You don't remember that bit?" Ryder, our resident goth model, asked. He had black, shoulder-length hair, black eyeliner around his brown eyes, and black clothes with chains.

Massive dick.

He always gave me a good ride.

I furrowed my brow. I barely remembered anything. "I have brief glimpses."

"You're going to get it annulled, right?" Sunny asked.

I shrugged. "Eventually." I liked the idea of being married. This was a fake one, but it was probably the only time in my life I would be wedded to anyone. Junkie, sex worker, porn stars weren't typically desirable to upstanding citizens like Lucas Black.

I knew I wasn't, for sure.

There was certainly no future for us. Love and family, and all that.

Carter was the only one I'd ever been in love with, and he had been as screwed up as I was at the time. I'm not sure where we'd be if we'd exchanged those three words.

Probably broken up and hating each other.

We were better off as best friends.

It was obvious that Lucas wouldn't even want to be friends with me. The look of revulsion on his face when he'd realized we were married would be forever etched on my mind.

He found me unpalatable in the extreme.

Michael, our producer, stormed in through the dressing room door. "Jet, get your ass in gear. We're filming in fifteen minutes. Studio A. Be there." Then stormed right back out.

"Gotta go." I winked at the group, then hit the showers. I had my enema bulb with me and used the warm water to fill it and clean away all traces of Lucas's cum from my ass.

Made me a little sad.

Scrubbed clean and hair blow-dried, I slipped on a jock strap. Two snorts of cocaine to clear my head, then I hurried down to Studio A. Through the curtains was a black wall with a table butted up against it where I'd be lying. I stayed out of camera shot until I was motioned over.

I arranged myself on the hard cushioning on the table, or bed if you could call it that, and fed my legs through an opening at my feet. I shuffled down until the drape shielding me from the other side came to rest on my abs. I obediently put my arms above my head when motioned to do so.

I looked straight up. The camera above me had a red light on. They were recording. The setup was all part of the scene. The guy attending to me put black leather handcuffs on me and clipped my hands to the board above my head, restraining me. Then disappeared.

Someone, likely the same guy, lifted my legs, grabbed me around the thighs, and tugged me down into a better position. My arms became stretched taut above my head.

I couldn't see what was happening with my bottom end, which meant my heart began hammering when my jock strap was stripped away, exposing my thickening cock and heavy balls.

I was going to ride on this feeling of vulnerability.

His hands on me again, the guy wrapped some rope around my left thigh and attached it to the board. He repeated the action on the other side. I closed my eyes and moaned softly when the guy took my cock and wrapped his lips around it, sucking and licking to make me harder.

He pulled away far too soon.

Next were anklets. More clips, and I was positioned in a perfect V shape. Completely defenseless with my hole on glorious display. The guy pumped my hard cock a few times.

I'd been looking forward to this scene for weeks.

I loved gay sex—loved it.

Every minute, in my youth, I spent at that camp for being *dirty and evil* hadn't put me off what my body wanted and needed, and what my mind desired. I was gay. Utterly and completely.

Mixed with a slutty personality, porn and prostitution were the distractions I needed.

On the other side of the wall came the sound of shuffling feet.

I'd agreed to fifteen men. Each fuck being marked on my thighs in permanent black marker. My cock bobbed as I squirmed. There was a quiet round of laughter at my desperation.

Then someone touched my thighs, followed by hot breath on my hole. I knew my ridged opening was already looking sloppy. Pretty sure the first guy to fuck me wouldn't care.

I arched my chest up as he licked and prodded and hummed as he ate my ass. Spitting and sucking, then introducing a finger. A slop of lube, and he soon had his fist in my ass, I was so loose. I groaned as each thrust and retreat shifted me up and back on the bed.

I whined when my ass was vacated. But it wasn't for long. His fist was soon replaced by his long, thick cock. He grasped onto my thighs and fucked me hard and fast, then filled me with cum.

My first load.

When he stepped away, I felt his deposit drool down my skin.

Mark one was made on the back of my thigh.

Guy number two's dick was short but fat, and he had good technique. He didn't last long. A second mark was drawn on my thigh. Three, four ... five. A quick hand job while I was being fucked, and I came all over my abs. I would have been happy to be denied the release.

By the time number fifteen came inside me, I was an oozing mess. And exhausted. But my day wasn't over yet. I had a client who liked to fuck me after I'd been gangbanged.

I felt dizzy, and my legs were shaking as I was untied. I took a second until I felt confident enough to swing my legs off the edge of the bed and sit. I sat there, propped on one hip to save my sore ass, for a few minutes until I'd recovered enough to leave Studio A.

After showering, I put on a white dress shirt and a slick grey suit, completed with some shiny black shoes. I would've looked like a million bucks if my eyes weren't dark and sullen.

I'd been at the drugs hard during the week. Didn't remember most of it. Vague recollections of Carter showing up to bathe me, dress me, and make me eat food.

I was pathetic and vile.

That's what my parents had called me when I struggled to control my shift from happening. It was strictly forbidden in the group of families we belonged to. I would be chained in the basement and starved until they deemed it was time to give me another chance to live up to their expectations.

They had made me feel revulsion for being a shifter.

I still struggled with it daily.

Needing to be revved up to survive the rest of my day, I did two long lines of cocaine off the hand dryer in the bathroom of the dressing room. I would hit the whisky hard at dinner.

The drugs, alcohol, and sex helped me to forget.

I dismissed my history.

I'd enjoyed the scene with the first nine or ten guys, but then it became work. Groaning, moaning, and begging for more on repeat. My ass was beaten up, numb, and leaking.

Just the way my *date* liked.

At least he was going to feed me first. I hadn't eaten much in the two days before the scene. Easier to clean the pipes that way, but I hadn't cleaned my ass in my second shower of the day.

Instead, I'd put on two pairs of underwear and a feminine napkin to keep the escaping cum from seeping through onto my dress slacks. The things I did for money.

In addition to keeping my ass swampy, Darryl, my client, would want me strung out on heroin when he fucked me. He liked me practically comatose. Not able to object to anything.

I would be an unresponsive piece of meat with a trashed, sloppy, cum-filled hole.

Then I'd get to sleep, $1000 richer overall for the day. I wouldn't need to work again until next weekend. It was a schedule I could work with. Drive out to Metro City on Friday night. Back in Creekside on Sunday. Then I had the rest of the week to feed my dirty habit to excess at home.

Drugs weren't cheap in Metro City. Police department crackdowns meant fewer dealers on the streets. Not sure why they cared, but it had driven prices up to triple what they were even a month ago. I was feeding a $1000 per week habit. I remembered the olden days of $500 per month.

I left the studio and took a cab to the high-end restaurant attached to a hotel—The Grand Metro. My client was loaded to the gills with money and never beat me.

Yet.

He was a rare treat.

Walking into the restaurant, I spotted Darryl at a dimly lit, intimate table near the window. Best table in the house. He always treated me good.

He smiled at me as I approached and stood while I took a seat.

Such a gentleman.

"So nice to see you, Jesse. It's been a few weeks."

I winked at him. "I wanted to make sure I could provide you with what you like."

His smile turned increasingly hungry. "And did you?"

"Fifteen loads."

Darryl's eyebrows rose. "Wow ... very nice. You must have such a pretty bloom."

"Pink, swollen, and wet the way you like me."

My date shifted in his seat, presumably to adjust his thickening cock.

"Did you bring your ... medicine?"

"Enough for two doses if you're feeling energetic."

Darryl smirked, then looked down at his menu. "I'm going to order you the cod on greens."

I wrinkled my nose. I wasn't a cod fan, but I didn't get to choose my dinner when I was out with Darryl. He liked to be in charge of everything. And he never let me eat anything heavy.

The concession was the continuous string of drinks he obliged me. He wanted me as fucked up as possible. He had a disturbing drugged rape kink that I was happy to go along with.

He talked *at* me about his work as a cardiothoracic surgeon—his patients' stories and how thankful they were that he had saved their lives in some cases. I let him brag, made all the right sounds, and faked exclamations of awe to inflate his arrogant confidence further.

I was feeling pretty good by the time we went up to the suite he'd reserved.

Once through the door, he was on me fast, his hands rough as he tore at my pants' button and fly. I obediently struggled and cried for help enough to make his aggression surge.

My pants and underwear around my hips, he tossed me on the bed and dug around in the soft leather satchel I carried with me until he located my heroin paraphernalia.

He surged at me and wrapped his fingers around my neck.

His voice was harsh in my ear. "Be a good boy and take a hit, or I'll break your neck."

I was legitimately shaking as I cooked. He'd never hurt me, but there was always a first time. Once my syringe was ready, I kicked off one shoe and sock and scooted up the bed.

His gaze was carnal and greedy as I injected my *medicine* into the top of my foot. He liked to see the empty syringe beside my head on the bed. I set it there as the warmth flowed through me.

My hazy awareness saw him crawl toward me, fully dressed, his hard dick out. All part of his fantasy. He tossed me onto my stomach and yanked my pants down around my knees, otherwise fully dressed.

I whimpered and pleaded with him to stop, then succumbed to a peaceful place.

I remember the grunting and swearing and being obliterated into the mattress and how I just took it, barely aware. Certainly not feeling any pain. Even if he decided to abuse me, I couldn't have stopped him. I was at his mercy. He *raped* me until he came, and his violent streak subsided.

After he was finished with me, he left, and I dug around in my satchel and located the golden wedding ring. I lay back on the bed, held up my hand, and slipped it back on my finger.

The marriage wasn't real, but it felt good at the moment.

Lucas was an amazing male. He'd treated Carter with patience and respect.

Any shifter would be lucky to have him as a mate.

Chapter 3

Lucas

Being at work with Carter on Monday morning after what Jesse and I had shared on the weekend, the carnal uninhibited sex and the impromptu marriage, was surreal.

Every time he looked at me, I blushed. He had to be wondering what the hell was wrong with me. I was usually stoic and dignified. Now, my attention kept wandering to images of Jesse.

Jesse kneeling on the bed, bent over, his hole ready for me to lick and suck and prod with my tongue, then plunge into with my cock. Jamming into him until we both came.

Jesse on his knees at my feet, looking up at me, blinking, as he sucked my cock.

God, his eyes were beautiful.

Jesse straddling me, bouncing on my dick, and throwing his head back in ecstasy.

I caught myself panting.

So much cum.

So much cocaine. I remembered that we'd continued the party in my hotel room. I hadn't had any cocaine, just more drinks, but Jesse had made a game of sniffing lines of coke off my body.

After doing a line off my hard cock, he'd sucked and licked away the residue.

The night with Jesse had been unhinged.

And we would soon bring it to a conclusion. I'd waited until today—Wednesday, after gathering enough courage to reveal my sordid story, and dashed off to my lawyer's on my lunch break. He raised an eyebrow, but carried on professionally to complete what I needed him to do.

Back on the worksite, tucked in my coat pocket was a single sheet of paper that would sever my marriage to Jesse. A lust-fueled night and a marriage that never should have happened.

I avoided bumping into Carter for the next hour because I was worried about the paper dropping onto the floor and Carter seeing it and asking questions. To alleviate the building stress, I took the document out to my truck and jammed it into the overstuffed glovebox, then went back inside and continued to behave like a live wire was attached to my chest; I was so jumpy.

I needed this to be over.

When we shut down the job for the night, I was prepared for what I had to do next. I hopped into my truck and drove to Jesse's cabin, the one that Carter and Rory paid for.

Jesse was too much of an addict to manage his own rent.

I needed to remember that.

So then, why was my heart beating so hard as I stood at his front door? It was thrumming away for stupid, *absolutely-not* reasons. More sex with Jesse was out of the question.

Lucas. Get a grip.

I was going to knock, but the door was ajar, so I tapped on it and opened it fully.

"Hello? Jesse?"

Across the foyer and into the living room, I could see him. His back end was seated on the sofa, but he was entirely folded in two, his messy hair touching his shoes, his arms hanging loose.

It was the most uncomfortable position I'd ever seen anyone in.

Seeing him like this—it struck me that I was entirely out of my depth. My idyllic life had not prepared me to see someone so incapacitated by drugs. I felt incredibly naïve.

I wasn't sure what to do.

I couldn't leave him like that, bent over like a soft noodle.

Jesse didn't stir when I went over to him and nudged his ribcage with my knee, so I caressed his back and shook him gently. He groaned but didn't move.

Fuck.

I was going to need to be more forceful. I grasped both of his shoulders and lifted him to a sitting position, and that's when he burst to life, turning angry eyes on me.

"What ... the ... fuck," he mumbled; barely decipherable.

I stepped back. "You were bent over. It must've been hard to breathe like that."

"Fuck ... right ... off." Jesse hauled himself off the sofa and stumbled toward the hallway. I could hear pictures being knocked off the wall as he made his way to who knows where.

I looked at the coffee table. Some foil, a bent spoon, a lighter, belt, and an uncapped needle were scattered on its surface. Among them was a randomly dumped pile of white pills.

I wondered which of them had rendered him practically comatose.

Maybe all of it.

I sighed with resignation and glanced around behind me to the kitchen. There wasn't a dirty dish or pot in sight. Either he was an extremely tidy drug addict, or he hadn't eaten in some time.

I was betting on the second of those.

Carter told me he kept Jesse's fridge stocked, so I wasn't surprised to find all the fixings for a sandwich inside. I set to work making one. Maybe I could get Jesse to eat it.

The sandwich made, I set the dirty knife in the sink and crossed my arms. He was taking too long. I wasn't even sure where he'd gone. I felt compelled to check on him and found him in the bathroom. He was wedged between the toilet and the tub, his face on the toilet seat, and he was drooling. I'm not sure how he managed to get himself in the awkward position.

I reached down, grabbed his arms, and hoisted him to his feet. He was like a rag doll—the urge to fight me no longer there. The only thing I could think to do was put him in bed.

I dragged him down the hall and found a bed that looked slept in. He was dead weight as I lay him on it and covered him with a blanket. I couldn't stop myself from touching him.

"Thanks," he muttered as I stroked his hair.

Why are you stroking his hair?

I stopped, but despite the state I found him in... here, resting peacefully, he looked angelic, as if the world had never taken advantage of him. Like all was well in his life.

My chest tightened.

I didn't want to leave him, but I needed to get home. Where my electrical business life ended, my life as pack leader started. I was run ragged most days. I switched off his lights and watched him from the doorway for a few moments, making sure his breaths were gentle and even.

I had to go.

The sandwich would have to wait. I wrapped it up and put it in the fridge, and hoped Jesse would find it later when he came around. I didn't know what else to do for him.

His signature to annul our marriage would have to wait for another day.

I hadn't even signed it yet.

I rubbed my chest as I started my truck.

My heart was bothered, and I didn't dare look to find out why.

The lawn out back of the community center looked like a fantasy land. It was evident that Shaun, not Carter, had organized the decorations for their spring commitment ceremony.

From where I was seated, I could see the back of Jesse's head. It had been over a week since I went by his cabin to have him sign the annulment document. Two weeks since the deed.

He appeared alert today and was dressed in a grey suit that made his shoulders look broad from behind. I was fixated on his neck, not listening to the vows that Carter had worked so hard on. I'd heard them before. He'd tortured me with version after re-written version for weeks.

I remembered kissing the back of Jesse's neck as I'd fucked his ass from behind. And his earlobes. I'd sucked on one until he squirmed and moaned for more.

He'd tasted like sweat and sin.

Jesse glanced over his shoulder at me.

He must have felt me staring.

Or maybe he'd detected the scent of my arousal.

I sucked in a fast breath when he gave me a wicked, wicked smile in full view of everyone in my vicinity. And damn if I didn't want to kiss those sultry lips right off his face.

I refocused on the words being spoken. It was Shaun's turn. His vows were beautiful. Their love was strong. I needed that in my life for myself and to become a better pack leader.

A pack leader was always more effective when they had their Omega mate at their side, sharing the role. Someone strong of mind and conviction. Someone ready to lead with me.

My Beta assistant, Clara, had been bringing me the names of possibilities. Mostly female Omega wolf shifters. Some males. All well-bred and prepared for a challenging pack role.

None of them appealed to me.

After the ceremony, I followed Jesse into the community center. There were long tables filled with food along one wall of the gymnasium that had been decorated to within an inch of its life in pink. I stepped up beside Jesse as he lifted a plate and started down the line.

I cleared my throat.

"Beautiful ceremony."

Someone bumped me, and my shoulder pressed up against Jesse's.

God, he smells good.

"It was," Jesse answered. "Found it hard to pay attention, though."

"Me too."

Jesse hummed, setting off my cock. "I wonder why?"

My heart quickened. "Exactly how hungry are you?"

Jesse chuckled. "For food? Not very. Do you have another idea?"

I set down my plate.

What are you doing?

"Follow me in a few seconds to outside Shaun's office." I hoped he knew where that was because I didn't wait for him to answer; my body focused on getting there.

Getting what it wanted.

I only had to wait a short time before Jesse's silhouette walked toward me in the dim light of the after-hours hallway. He was immediately in my personal space, holding my face.

I closed my eyes as his lips covered mine, so sweet and tender. Then the heat increased, and I wrapped my arms around him as the kiss turned into a battle to overpower one another.

I pulled away, grabbed Jesse by the front of his shirt, and hauled him across the hall and into the men's bathroom. We were a tangle of arms and legs as we danced, stumbling, into a stall.

Jesse slammed and locked the door, and then his frantic, seeking hands were on me. I endeavored to consume him as I kissed him. I wanted to possess every molecule of his body.

I wanted Jesse.

I *needed* him.

I spun him to face the wall, stepped up close behind him, pinning him, and with more aggression than I'd ever used before, I reached around and hauled and yanked to undo his pants.

I growled as they dropped to the floor, and kissed the back of his neck, inhaling every intoxicating scent on his skin and hair, then sucked on his earlobe. I nibbled on it, making Jesse moan while I undid my pants and released my rock-hard cock. I pulled his underwear down past his ass. One swift movement, and I thrust past his tight hole and sank into him.

Jesse groaned, then chuckled.

He was throwing down a challenge. I rocked back and then up into him, piercing him high. Jesse released a string of obscenities as I fucked him, my body embodying my inner beast, desperate to fuck him into oblivion. I'd spent too much time imagining taking him like this.

Jesse slammed both his hands onto the wall as I pounded into him. The metal wall of the stall rattled and shook with each thrust. He was wearing the damned wedding ring on his ring finger.

"You need to take that off," I growled in his ear.

"No."

I used my forearm to keep him flat against the wall and drilled him harder, nearly lifting him off his feet. I wanted to fuck the life out of him. Why was he wearing the ring?

Each battering thrust brought me closer to climax.

He arched his back and bounced on my cock, jamming my dick deeper.

There ... right there. I set my teeth on his suit material close to the claiming area of his shoulder, then came so hard, I howled, not caring if anyone heard me.

I kept pumping my hips until my cock was finished filling him. Then I let it slip free of his ass. Jesse immediately turned, dropped to his knees, and took my dick into his mouth.

Such a dirty, dirty bear.

I ran my hand into his hair as he bobbed on my dick, cleaning it. He used his left hand to hold my shaft, keeping me somewhat stiff. He looked up at me with his gorgeous blue eyes.

Why is he still wearing the ring?

Jesse rose to his feet and kissed me. I pushed him against the wall and enjoyed the feel and taste of his mouth as I grasped his dick and pumped it until he came in my hand.

My fist coated, I started by smearing some of his cum on his lips, then I cleaned the rest off my hand with my tongue. Jesse looked delectable as he licked his lips, eating his seed.

One more kiss.

I wrapped my arms around his waist. He draped his around my neck. This kiss was slower and gentler, as if this encounter was leading to something more.

The ring.

I reluctantly left his lips.

"You need to take that ring off."

Jesse shook his head. "I'm not taking it off until it's over between us."

I'm sorry ... what?

"Stop fucking around, Jesse. Nothing is happening between us."

He tipped his head.

"Isn't it? You suggested this quick fuck. You're obviously not done with me."

I grunted. He was right. Fucking him hadn't got him out of my system. I wanted to take him home to my bed and ravish him without worrying about time or place.

Treat him like the special, beautiful, and sexy creature he was.

Where does that leave us?

"Jesse?"

Fuck. I stepped back from Jesse. I'd recognize Carter's voice anywhere; we'd spent so many hours together talking as we worked. And now we'd been caught by him post-fuck.

I'd known it was risky hauling Jesse into a bathroom stall.

That had been part of the lusty thrill.

"Busy, Carter," Jesse said. "Do your business and leave."

"Who's in there with you?"

"Not kissing and telling, Carter."

"More like fucking and telling. This is my ceremony of commitment to Shaun, and here you are in a bathroom stall getting your rocks off. You have no respect for me, asshole."

"Bullshit. Now, finish and leave, so we're not stuck in here, Carter."

Carter huffed and snorted, then used the urinal. While he was washing his hands, Jesse cupped my face and pressed a subtle kiss to my lips, reconnecting us.

I pressed my forehead to his, keeping our lips close.

"You are completely unravelling me," I whispered against his hot breath.

Jesse smiled. "Then my plan is working."

I chuckled and kissed him. "Maybe so, but this ends here. Take the ring off."

"I don't believe you. It's *not* over between us."

Carter knocked on the stall door. "Okay, I'm leaving."

"Good riddance," Jesse mumbled.

"Fuck off," was the reply.

The bathroom door opened, then closed with a thud. Jesse and I could talk about this another time. We needed to get back to the reception before Carter figured out who was missing.

We took a moment to fix our clothes.

I opened the stall door.

For fuck's sake.

Carter was leaning against the far wall with his arms crossed. His eyebrows rose. He'd only pretended to leave. I walked past him without a word to wash my hands.

I was going to let Jesse handle this.

"Okay, now what?" Jesse glared at Carter. "You caught us."

"How long has this been going on?"

"That's none of your business."

"I caught my boss fucking you. Pretty sure that affords me some explanation."

I turned, rested my ass against the counter, and crossed my arms. "Maddox's stag night."

Jesse smirked. "We spent the night doing all sorts of nasty things to each other."

I wasn't sure what Carter was thinking, but the ice picks he threw at Jesse with his eyes were an undeniable hint. Then his gaze tracked down Jesse's body to his left hand.

He rushed at Jesse, grabbed his hand, and jerked it up.

"What the fuck is this?"

"It's a ring."

"I can see that, but why is it on your ring finger?"

Then, as easy as telling someone his name ... "Lucas and I got married."

"I'm sorry ... you did what with my *boss*, Lucas?"

I pushed off from the counter. "It was an accident." I didn't want to get further involved in a conversation that I sensed would get more personal between the two of them.

They barely registered my leaving.

I could hear them arguing all the way down the hall. Carter felt betrayed because Jesse hadn't told him about me, and Jesse was refusing to take off the ring, declaring it wasn't over.

I reached into my pocket.

The metal ring was warm from being next to my body. I stroked it a few times. I was finding it impossible to dispose of something that symbolized the closeness between Jesse and me, the kind that led us to decide to marry. However drunken and deranged the decision had been, we'd felt something. I wished I could remember more of that part of our night.

All I could remember was the sex, the chapel, and that I had told Jesse I loved him.

For fuck's sake, Lucas.

The document for our annulment was stuffed in my glove box, becoming worse for wear after being shoved between a stack of napkins and the user manual.

It was going to stay there for a little longer.

Jesse was right.

I wasn't done with him yet.

What am I getting myself into?

I was in my office later that night when my carrier, Adam, knocked on my door and came in, and took a seat on the opposite side of my desk. He looked concerned. Had he heard the news of my indiscretions? I'd kept it out of our telepathic pack murmurings. Didn't mean he didn't know.

"What brings you out so late at night?" I asked.

Adam's jaw clenched, then his brow furrowed. "What's up with you?"

"What do you mean?"

"You've been acting strange. Clara brought it to your sire's attention."

Clara was my right hand. She'd served my sire, Lucas Sr., for many years and then my brother Maddox. She would've tried to dig out the details of my distraction from anyone who would talk to her, which is why she was so valuable to me as pack leader.

"I'm finding time management difficult."

Adam tipped his head. "You're the most organized wolf I know."

I sighed. "Fine. I'm having trouble in my personal life. I know something needs to end, but my heart is sending different messages. Delusional messages."

"With a potential mate?"

I laughed. "Absolutely not. He is not pack leader material."

"Then why can't you end it? You need a capable Omega by your side."

I grunted. "He's not even an Omega." That's all Adam was getting. There was no way I was telling him the male picking away at my heart was a bear. Certainly not that he was a drug addict.

"I'm not sure why you'd continue with him. You need to have pups."

I knew that. If I didn't pass the leadership to one of my siblings, the next leader of the East Creekside wolf pack would be one of my offspring. That's the way things had always been done.

Then why the hesitation?

Chapter 4

JESSE

The food in my belly felt good. Carter had made me a beef curry, cleaned up the kitchen, and was now sitting in the bathroom with me as I attempted to bathe myself to his standards.

My last clean had been on Sunday at the porn studio. It was Friday now, and I needed to get my head on straight and organized so I could drive to Metro City for a date with a client.

"Not sure you should be driving anywhere," Carter said.

"I've barely used anything in hours. I'm just tired."

"Hence, it is not a good idea to drive your motorcycle for four hours."

"I have a date at eight tonight. I need to leave by three." Which is probably why Carter had left work early. I'd told him this weekend's schedule. It was a full one.

"Maybe I should drive you."

"Don't be ridiculous. I'll be fine." I dumped a load of shampoo into my hand and plopped it on the top of my head. Carter moved from the toilet and knocked my hands away.

"Let me do that. You always do such a shit job."

I closed my eyes and hummed as he washed my hair. I loved how our relationship had evolved. Where we were now, it was the perfect mix of aggression and tenderness.

I wasn't in love with Carter anymore, but I loved him.

My hair done, Carter left me to dry off and slip into a simple t-shirt and jeans. Tonight's date wanted to meet me at Metro Lotus Gym. We'd work out for a while, him watching me, then hit the communal showers, where I'd wash my body in seductive strokes for his hungry enjoyment.

He liked that other men were looking at me.

Some with disgust ... others with appreciation.

Then we'd fuck in a dressing cubicle, and $250 would be mine.

When I emerged from my bedroom, Carter was straightening up the living room, folding blankets, arranging cushions, and picking up my liquor bottles to put away.

I'd be lost without him.

Out of habit, I spun my wedding ring around as I watched him. He caught the action as he walked past me. "Why do you keep that thing on? You're not really married."

I shrugged. "It makes me feel normal, like I don't have the sordid life I'm leading. Like someone loves me for me." Lucas didn't love me, but he had certainly accepted me where I was.

Or had he?

My mood saddened. I had a ghost of a memory of him telling me he loved me.

But he'd been drunk.

Last weekend, though, neither of us had been drunk or on anything at the community center. As far as I knew, that fuck had been completely clear-headed, *and* it wasn't an accident this time.

"I love you for you."

"You know what I mean. Lucas bothers to connect with me. I can imagine it's more."

"You think it's about more than sex?"

"I don't know ... maybe. He kisses me like I mean something to him."

"How much does he know?"

"If I shared my history with him, I don't think he remembers. Lucas would have questions, I know he would. I think he actually cares about me, Carter."

I had a vague recollection of Lucas rescuing me from the bathroom, putting me to bed, and lulling me to sleep by stroking my hair. If he didn't care, he wouldn't do stuff like that.

I'd even found a fresh sandwich in the fridge when hunger reared its head. But I was getting ahead of myself. I was a drug addict, and Lucas didn't need someone like me around.

"What about the dating and porn?"

I shook my head. "Again, if I did, he doesn't remember." And if I told him? Then what? I doubted he would want to touch me again. Lucas was too good for me.

My life was utterly filled with male aggression and the beratement and humiliation I'd tried to escape from. At sixteen, I'd run from it but found it again on the streets of Metro City.

There was no escape.

A shiver ran up my spine, and my mind exploded with images. The first time my incisors had descended, I'd been at the dinner table. I was eleven. I'd been a late bloomer.

For some reason, the smell of the roast beef had done it. My inner bear had wanted out. Even my claws began to show. I fought hard to reverse both, but it was impossible.

My dad erupted, swearing at me to stop. His anger threw me off, making me want to shift even more to protect myself from danger. I was fighting a raging battle when he raced around the table, grabbed my shirt, and hauled me down the stairs to the basement.

It was the first time I'd seen the space. I wasn't allowed down there. Bear shifters often came and went from it during the night. I could hear them grunting and growling through the door.

My dad pushed me up against a wooden frame in the form of an X and yanked my pants down. I closed my eyes as I waited. For some reason, I knew what was coming.

I grimaced and gritted my teeth through the thrashing of my tender young skin. Covered in welts that felt raised and painful on my ass, I was surprised when my dad shackled me to a wall.

Even more surprised when he left me there for three sunrises and night falls with nothing but a bowl of water, an old, musty mattress, and a narrow glimpse of the sky. I was starving and scared, and I wondered where my mom was and why she wasn't saving me.

Day three, and my dad came down with a folded belt in his hands and released me. Back against the wooden frame, he struck my bare ass covered in welts with the belt. After each strike, I was ordered to scream *I will not shift* repeatedly until I was wailing in pain.

I didn't shift for weeks after that, but eventually my body won out again, and I was right back down in the basement, this time for four days—this time without the protection of clothes.

I'd been so cold down there.

Carter touched my shoulder. "Are you all right?"

My Alpha male tendencies forced me to stand straight and give off an air of confidence. I'd never told Carter about my past. I'd been his Alpha. My job had been to protect him.

Even with our new roles as best friends, I would never tell him. It would make him worry about me even more. My sordid life with drugs, alcohol, and sex was enough for him to deal with.

"Exhausted."

"Reschedule your date. Stay here tonight. Start fresh in the morning."

I sighed. Carter was right. "Maybe."

I was about to see Carter out when a big pickup truck pulled up outside our cabin, and I detected a familiar and welcome scent.

Lucas.

"What's he doing here?" Carter asked.

"Probably wants me to sign the annulment papers."

Carter gripped my shoulders. "Please do it. And take that ring off. You're torturing yourself by pretending your time with Lucas means anything." He waited for me to nod.

He released me and opened the front door as Lucas was about to knock. Lucas had a ragged-looking piece of paper in his hand. Its existence really was the reason he was here.

It gave me heart palpitations.

I didn't want to sign it.

And not just because he was gorgeous with his luscious dark hair, sultry brown eyes, and crimson full lips that were incredible to kiss. It didn't even bother me that he towered above me.

I didn't want to sign it because I wasn't ready for the dream to end.

"I'll leave you to it," Carter said as he let Lucas in and left the cabin.

We stood there, staring at each other for a few moments. Lucas lifted the paper. "I've brought this for you to sign." Reluctantly, I took it from him and read it.

It was straightforward. The annulment text outlined that we were different species of shifter and that the marriage had been a drunken accident. I read it through to the last line.

And down to the signature area.

I looked up at Lucas.

"You haven't signed it."

Lucas crossed his arms. "I wanted you to sign it first."

"Why?"

He grunted, and his face turned crimson. "To make sure you want to."

I studied his eyes. They were pleading with me, but pleading for what? Soft and sad and barely blinking. Even his posture was off. His shoulders were slumped, his Alpha sullen.

"What if I said I'm not signing it?"

Lucas stepped closer to me and cupped my face. "Then I'd do this."

I quite honestly swooned with the kiss he laid on me. So tender and caring and hot all at the same time. He yearned for me as much as I desired his touch.

This wasn't over between us.

Without a word, I took one of his hands from my face and broke the kiss, then led him down the hallway to my bedroom. This wasn't a bathroom stall, and we weren't drunk.

This time would mean something.

Lucas kissed me down onto the mattress, and I was infinitely thankful that Carter had changed my bedding for me. The comforter had a lavender scent that he liked to spray on it.

I raised my hands over my head, squirming with building need, as Lucas peeled off my shirt and tossed it onto the end of the bed. Then he was back on my mouth, kissing me until I felt like a languishing puddle that would take any form he wanted of me.

His lips moved from mine to my jawline, up to my ear—tugging and teasing. Then down the side of my neck to my collarbone. He licked and sucked on it until I thrust my hips upward, desperate to be closer to him. He chuckled as he moved to the other side, then down to my nipple.

The flicking with his tongue and sucking of each hard nub made me arch my back and run my hands through his hair, clinging to him. Lucas was taking his time, and I loved him for it.

No one took their time with me.

No one cared enough about me to make me feel good.

He slipped onto his knees between my legs and worked on opening my jeans. I was soon lifting my ass so he could dispense with them and my underwear.

Lucas brushed his hands up and down my thighs as he nudged my balls with his nose while inhaling and growling quietly. He was gentle as he sucked one of my balls into his mouth.

He hummed around it, lathering it up with spit, then suckled on it.

My cock bobbed, and I closed my eyes. Lucas was treating me with such reverence. Like he thought I was special. Maybe even that I deserved to be taken care of.

I'd always been the Alpha with Carter, even during our *mating*. Because that's what I was. I used to take care of him. He was always eager to bring me pleasure, but not like this.

Lucas wrapped his palm around my cock and attended to it so tenderly, sucking, licking, and running his lips up and down my shaft. He pumped it a few times, then released it to crawl up my body and capture my mouth again. He only stopped to let me scoot up the bed while he removed his clothes. What he revealed was a tall, muscular beast of a wolf shifter.

So gorgeous, I couldn't believe he was spending time with me.

Back on me, he kissed my lips, my jaw, each eyelid. I raised my hands above my head to rest on the headboard. His gaze landed on the inside of my arms and the noticeable track marks—old pink and white scars up and down my collapsed veins I'd been forced to stop using.

He didn't recoil. He didn't even look disgusted or scared.

Instead, Lucas did the most moving thing. He straddled my hips, held my arm, and kissed the marred skin from elbow to wrist. He looked into my eyes, then switched to the other side.

What I saw in that fleeting moment was a dose of ardent warmth.

Maybe, just maybe, this tumble in the sheets meant more to Lucas than simply sex.

I wrapped my legs around his waist when he moved to be between my thighs. I switched off the Alpha part of my brain. The first time I'd let a male fuck me had been difficult. I'd wanted to lead. I'd wanted to be the one to penetrate. Bottoming went against my Alpha nature.

Now, I found peace in it.

Lucas positioned his thick cockhead at my hole and kissed me as he eased past my tight ring. I groaned and tipped my chin up. There was no need to open me up first. I was as receptive as an Omega. Even created enough slickness to remove the need for lube. All things Lucas either remembered from his hotel room or our fast fuck in the cubicle.

He sighed, sending a warm, rolling gush of air past my lips.

I gripped his back as he stuffed my ass, and his abundant pubic hairs tickled my balls. I embraced him to keep him close to me as he tipped his hips back, creating a dark void.

I dug my fingers into his hair, my other hand on his ass to ride his thrust into me, and lifted my hips to take him in fully. Lucas rocked back, then plunged in and out, bringing me to a place no one, other than Carter, had ever done. I felt unconditionally loved.

I looked up into his warm, seductive eyes. They were focused on mine. With each thrust, both of our mingling breaths quickened. Neither of us looked away. I cupped his jawline.

He was feeling it, too. The unmistakable tension of two beings fooling themselves if they thought this was a simple fuck. I sealed my lips to his in short bursts, so I wouldn't lose sight of his eyes looking down at me. I held his face in both hands. He moved his hand to caress my cheek.

Three crazy little words danced on my tongue.

I kissed him harder instead and sighed and grunted as I spilled and slicked up the space between us. He was only seconds behind me. He growled, then howled as he came.

I tipped my head to one side when his descending incisors scraped across the skin between my neck and my shoulder. I knew what it meant. Wolves claimed each other by biting them there.

Then pronounced to their pack that they had found their mate.

He was fighting hard not to bite me.

I kept his head there as he sucked and gnashed in frustration instead.

Lucas kissed my cheek, then rolled, taking me with him. He played with my facial hair beneath my cheekbones as I relaxed my full weight on top of him. He was so much bigger than me. I attributed my smaller size to the fact that I hadn't been permitted to shift in my growing years.

"You're gorgeous," Lucas whispered as he studied my eyes.

I kissed his chin. "So are you."

Lucas sighed. "Jesse ... what are we doing?"

"I don't know. We can't seem to keep our hands off one another." My Alpha re-emerged, not wanting to be so effeminate, so I moved to lie beside Lucas, equal in dominance.

"This has to be the last time," Lucas said.

"I know."

"We both need to sign the annulment."

I grunted, unsure if I should speak. I felt needy, but I said it anyway. "Give me another week."

Lucas rolled to face me. "Why?"

I didn't feel the need to censor myself around Lucas. "I'll never be married for real. I'm no one's fantasy mate. I'd be surprised if I were still alive in five years."

Lucas touched my chest. "Don't say that."

Reality rushed in, and I sat up, knocking his hand aside, and swung my legs off the bed. "It's the truth, Lucas." When he touched my back, I jerked away from him. I was playing a stupid game with him. He didn't want to stay married to me. Why would he? I was trash.

The self-deception needs to stop.

I wrenched the ring off my finger, tossed it at him, and took off from my bedroom. I went straight to the kitchen, found a pen, and signed the document sitting on the coffee table.

The delusion was over.

I hid in the bathroom until I heard Lucas leave. I couldn't face him. I didn't want to see the relief on his face when he saw that I'd signed my name to annul our marriage.

It would crush me.

Back in my bedroom, I looked at my phone.

I still had time to make it to my 8 p.m. date.

CHAPTER 5

LUCAS

I was going to be late coming back from lunch, but the line at the courthouse was longer than I'd expected. Each person who approached the lone clerk had a story to tell as they submitted whatever documents they were filing. Finally, it was my turn.

"What can I help you with?"

I set the seriously disheveled document containing Jesse's signature on the counter. It had spent another week in my glovebox and was taking on the look of an antiquity.

"I want to file this annulment."

The woman read the document and turned it back to face me.

"You're missing a signature."

"Yeah, that would be mine." I wiped my damp hands off on the front of my jeans. My mind was still screeching back and forth, trying to decide what I wanted to do.

She handed me a pen. "Put your signature on there, and I'll get this filed for you."

I poised the pen over the line and started the first part of my signature. The automatic forward momentum of my hand ceased, and the thudding of my heart told me I was doing the wrong thing.

The how and why weren't clear.

I set down the pen and picked up the paper. "I changed my mind."

"Fine." The woman looked past my shoulder. "Next."

I shoved my way past the line and through the doors to the outside. I looked down at the paper. Jesse had been clear with what he wanted, but I wasn't sure of his reasons. It felt as though we'd made an intense pact while I was moving in him. The look in his eyes—the softness of his open mouth as his quickening breaths rushed past his lips. I wanted more time with him.

I folded the paper in four, tore it into strips, and dropped it into a litter bin.

One simple act, and I was able to breathe again.

The last time I stayed at the Grand Metro in Metro City, my entire world changed. This time, I was meeting my brother Maddox to satisfy our need to see one another in person.

I hadn't seen him since his wedding a month ago.

The restaurant was dimly lit and intimate—everything I needed to calm my nerves. I had stuff I wanted to talk to my big brother about. I hoped he would have the advice I needed.

Maddox took a sip of his whisky as he looked across the table at me.

"Something is bothering you," he said. "You were distracted all through dinner."

I set down my glass of water. "I need your counsel on something."

"Pack stuff?"

"No, personal." I let out a long sigh as I gathered my nerve. "What would you do if you knew someone with multiple substance addictions? How would you help them?"

Maddox tapped on his glass, which sat on the table. "You can't do anything but support them."

I frowned. "How do you mean?"

"You can't guide someone to get help. They need to want to do it. It's not on you. If they want to go into recovery, it has to be their idea. You can't try to coerce them. It won't work."

That was *not* what I wanted to hear, but it's what I had read on the internet as well.

"Even if you care deeply for one another?"

"You can't cure them, Lucas. That has to come from within them."

I spun my water glass and looked around the restaurant. In the far corner, near the window, sat two males. One obviously wealthy and cultured, and the one facing him—familiar.

I recognized the back of that neck.

I'd stared at it long enough at Carter and Shaun's commitment ceremony.

I looked down past the bottom of their tablecloth. Jesse had his foot out of his shoe, and he was rubbing it up and down the calf of the human male, who was looking at him hungrily.

My heart sank.

Jesse had a boyfriend.

I felt like an idiot. Pining after him and ripping up the annulment document. Of course, he had signed it. Jesse already had someone special in his life. And it wasn't me.

Then why had he slept with me?

Why the loving looks and quick breaths with words of affection dancing on them?

I hadn't been imagining it.

The back of my neck bristled, and Maddox's words of concern from across the table went unacknowledged. I was feeling rage and jealousy. I leapt to my feet and crossed the room.

Jesse turned before I had even reached them, catching my scent. He looked startled and worried—and panicked. He hadn't expected me to ever find him like this.

He abandoned the male's leg and slipped his foot back in his shoe.

I stepped right up to the table and glared at Jesse's boyfriend, knowing my Alpha wolf shifter size would intimidate his mere human one. I was dismissive as I looked at him.

I'm not sure what Jesse saw in him.

He was at least twenty years older than Jesse and bald.

I turned my attention away from him and onto Jesse.

"I'm glad I found you," I said, not knowing where I was going with this but determined to see it through. I needed him away from this male. "You need to come with me."

"Why?"

I grasped an idea out of the air. "Carter is in Metro City, and he's in trouble."

Jesse whipped his phone out of his pocket and checked for messages, then stared up at me. It took him a second to decide to play along. He looked across the table at his boyfriend.

"Sorry, Darryl, I have to go. Can we reschedule for tomorrow night?"

"I can't. I'm on call."

Jesse stood. "Then Sunday. I'll make it extra special for you."

"Okay. We meet in my room at eight. No later. I want at least six hours out of you."

I scowled at the male. What the hell was he talking about?

Jesse nodded. "Of course. Thank you."

The male grunted, and Jesse turned from the table, gripped my arm, and hauled me across the restaurant to the entrance of the hotel. "What the fuck, Lucas? You just cost me $500."

What?

My vision narrowed in on the male in the far room. He wasn't Jesse's boyfriend. He was Jesse's client. I growled and took a step back into the restaurant. I wanted to rip his obnoxious face and his upper-class torso and limbs into minuscule bloody pieces.

Jesse gripped my lapels hard to stop me.

"Alpha ... calm down."

Maddox joined Jesse in holding me back from what might have turned into a blood bath that landed me in jail for life. I didn't want anyone touching Jesse like he was an object.

"Alpha, please." Jesse put his hands on my chest and gave me a shove. His body wasn't strong enough to subdue me, but with Maddox's help, I didn't have a choice but to stand down.

Jesse touched my face. "Lucas, please ... for me. He doesn't matter. He means nothing." With those words, my brother backed away, leaving me in Jesse's care, and furrowed his brow at me.

He didn't say a word.

He'd given me his two cents. Now he knew who my concerns were about and that there was history between us. History that prompted Jesse to take my hand and lead me across the lobby.

There was a tense phone call with my brother in my future.

"Do you have a hotel room?" Jesse asked.

I gave him my full attention. "Yeah. Nothing special, though."

"It'll be special because you're in it."

I wasn't sure where this was leading. But historically, it would end with me filling Jesse with my seed; my body desperate to make him my mate and put a pup in him.

That's not what this was.

I wasn't sure what this was.

We took the elevator, then I led him down to my room. When I tried to kiss him after closing the door, he stepped back and shook his head. One strong inhalation told me why.

"How many males have you been with today?" I asked.

"I counted ten." Jesse looked at the floor. "But it could've been more."

Jesse.

My Jesse.

I needed to know more if he'd tell me.

"Where? Why?"

Jesse stared into my eyes. "I work for a gay porn studio. I did a group scene today. Which is why I was on a date with Darryl. He likes to fuck me after that many males have filled me."

Swear to God, I'm going to kill that human.

I wrinkled my nose, a low growl rumbling in my chest.

"And who is Darryl to you?"

"A well-paying client."

"You're an escort."

"I am ... I need the money. Drugs aren't cheap."

My anger disappeared.

The scent of all those males on Jesse and his story made me feel as if my heart was being crushed. I wasn't mad at him. I didn't feel sorry for him. All I felt was a need to care for him.

Soothe him.

Make him feel loved.

"I'd like to wash you."

Jesse's eyebrows peaked. "Like a bath ... or get in the shower *with* me kind of wash?"

Sex was *almost* the last thing on my mind.

"I want to clean their scent from your skin."

Jesse tipped his head. "I'd like that."

"Good." I walked past him, went into the bathroom, and started the tub filling. He appeared at the bathroom door, looking up at me with his gorgeous eyes, and began undressing.

My fingers longed to touch his bare skin, but I didn't. When the tub was full and steaming, Jesse stepped into it and immersed himself, spending a moment with his face under water.

When he emerged, he smiled up at me.

"I thought for sure you were going to kill Darryl."

"I don't like the idea of him touching you."

"You went full-blown aggressive Alpha."

I stroked his cheek, relieved he was here in my room with me. "I care about you."

"What about the annulment?"

I took my time, breathing through what I wanted to say. "I tore it up."

His eyebrows rose. "You did what?"

"I didn't sign it. I shredded it and tossed it in the garbage outside the courthouse."

"You got as far as the courthouse."

"Right up to the counter." I brushed my fingers from Jesse's cheek down to his shoulder. He leaned his head against my hand and stroked my wrist.

"We're not finished yet," he said.

I shook my head. "Every molecule in me says *no*."

Jesse looked up at me. "Wash me, take me to bed, and hold me. No sex ... all right?"

My chest tightened, but I knew Jesse was right. We couldn't fall into having sex every time we were in the same place together. There needed to be more between us than that.

But I wasn't sure there would be.

"I promise."

I soaped up a washcloth and started with Jesse's shoulders. The more I scrubbed, the more I realized there was cum all over his skin. Its existence and Jesse's need to do that kind of work to buy street drugs made me feel ill. I didn't want this life for him.

Any of it.

He was too precious.

Tears threatened to spill down my cheeks as I dried every part of him, taking my time, and lavishing him with as much loving attention as I could gather ....

While on the verge of having a breakdown.

Every touch was my best, but not nearly enough care for the amount he deserved.

I kept my word and slipped beneath the sheets in my jockey shorts with Jesse and pulled his back to my chest. I settled in against his clean hair with my nose and nuzzled him.

I dismissed the fact that he had slipped a pink pill into his mouth moments before.

"I'm a sex worker, and I do gay porn," Jesse said quietly, reminding me.

"I understand that." I kissed the back of his head. "Not going to say I'm okay with it, or that I understand it, but it's not for me to tell you what to do with your life."

"I need the money every week for drugs. I work flat out on the weekends."

I hugged him tighter.

"I don't understand why you're here with me," he added.

A coil built in my gut, wanting me to move. To get off that bed and do what my heart was telling me to do. I fought the urge, not fully understanding what I'd be getting into with Jesse.

My heart won out.

"Give me a second." I kissed his head and climbed out of bed. In my wallet were two objects that were causing the leather to stretch. I took them out, went back to the bed, and knelt on the floor where Jesse could see me. I reached for his left hand and took it in mine.

His gaze wandered from my eyes to my lips and back again.

The words I spoke to him would mean something to us both. I set both wedding rings on the bed and lifted his slightly smaller one and slid it onto his ring finger.

He blinked, tears gathering in his eyes.

"I want to stay married," I told him.

Jesse sucked in a breath and nodded, then took the other ring off the bed. He held out his hand for mine. It felt like the world fell back into place when he returned the ring to my finger.

I crawled back behind him and held him, and we spent the entire night basking in whatever union we had agreed to. I had no idea what it was going to look like.

And how difficult it was going to be.

Because I wasn't stupid, Jesse was going to put me through hell. I knew that much. If I were looking for soft and fluffy, I wouldn't have taken this path.

I just wanted to be there for him.

I longed to be a haven he could count on.

CHAPTER 6

JESSE

I'm sure I'd been lying here for days on a dirty mattress. It was a regular haunt for me, this cold, derelict house, and someone was keeping me topped up with all the drugs I needed to erase the thoughts going through my head. But now I was on the other side, staring up at the ceiling.

Lucas had told me he wanted to stay married.

He'd put my ring back on my finger.

His was back on, too.

I held up my hand and turned it until my ring caught the light. I'd told Lucas what my life looked like, and he hadn't asked me to stop. Deep down, I wished he had, but my mind knew it wouldn't have made a difference. Drugs ruled my life. I woke up wanting them, and I went to sleep having taken them. I would've vehemently dismissed any request of his for me to quit.

I tucked my coat tighter around me. For the beginning of summer, Metro City was cold and miserable. The sun rarely shone here. The constant rain kept it from warming up.

I shivered. My feet were like blocks of ice. I'd had my shoes off for days, using the depleting veins for injection sites. Seeking a different kind of sedation, I'd switched to ketamine for variety, to mix things up a little. Parting from Lucas after a night in his arms had been hard.

I'd headed straight here, not wanting to deal with my emotions.

I set my left hand over my heart.

Despite my efforts to stop it, my heart had begun to beat for him. It didn't matter how many drugs I took; I always came back to the same conclusion. I needed Lucas in my life.

I sat up and waited for my light-headedness to subside, then pulled on my socks and boots. The design of my motorcycle boots meant that the top of my feet hurt because of the bruising.

It was going to be a long ride home.

I dug my phone out of my dress pants and scrolled through the messages. Darryl had blown up my phone. I'd missed our date, and he was beyond angry. I was going to need to submit to some of his more degrading and unusual kinks to make up for ghosting him.

I sent him a text to set up a date for Friday. Told him I'd been gang raped in a back alley by a group of men and crashed at a drug den to forget the horrific ordeal. He'd like that story.

Darryl was a sick fuck, but he paid well.

I stared at the beginning of the thread of messages Lucas had sent me. It said, *"Looking forward to seeing you again."* I opened the rest of it. *"Thinking of you."*

A tear ran down my cheek. Lucas was so innocent, caring, and kind, and he made me feel loved. How could I put him through the nightmare that was my life? I'd been lying here in my own filth, my pants and the mattress absorbing my lack of attempt to find a corner to piss in.

I read more.

"Loved holding you."

"I'm happy we're still married."

I didn't deserve this wolf. He was the pillar of the Creekside community. The leader of the East Creekside wolf pack. He had responsibilities. People looked up to him.

Who was I?

A nobody. A chain around his neck that would drag him down.

But he wanted me in his life—a relationship with me beyond physical. I couldn't simply file that away in the archives and leave it there unexplored.

I needed to talk to Carter.

I needed my best friend, and five hours later, after I figured out where I had parked my motorcycle, I pulled up outside the hardware store on Main Street in Creekside.

Phoning first had crossed my mind, but I wasn't sure I would follow through on heading to Carter and Shaun's, where I'd lay out all that had been happening between Lucas and me.

I knocked on their door, and Carter immediately opened it.

"Fuck, you stink," is the first thing he said to me.

"I've been deep under for a few days." I crossed my arms. "That's not why I'm here."

"Figured." He stepped back and let me into the kitchen. Shaun was sitting at the table, eating, and their apartment smelled like lavender and beef. My stomach grumbled, hungry.

Shaun rose from his seat. "I'll give you some time alone."

"Thanks, Shaun," Carter replied.

I looked at the floor. I'd rather Shaun weren't here. I dared to look Carter in the eyes after Shaun left. I'm sure I resembled a hellscape of drug use and broken sleep.

"I'd ask you to sit, but I don't want you making the sofa smell like a sewer."

I exhaled in resignation. I could stand. "I ran into Lucas in Metro."

"What did *ran into* entail?"

"He almost went Alpha on Darryl but took me to his hotel room instead."

Carter sighed. "You have got to *stop* having sex with him."

"I didn't ... we didn't. He bathed me and just held me in bed."

"And that made you feel something." Carter crossed his arms.

"I signed the annulment paper last week, but he didn't file it. He tore it up." I stuffed my hands in my pockets. "He said he wants to stay married to me. We put our rings back on."

Carter's eyebrows rose. "So, what does that mean?"

I shook my head. "I don't know, but he wants to spend more time with me."

"He hasn't seen you at your worst, Jesse."

"Actually, he has. A few weeks ago, he showed up at the cabin. My memory is dicey, but I know he tucked me into bed, stroked my hair, and made me a sandwich."

"So, you're back to wearing the wedding ring."

I pulled my hand out of my pocket and showed him. "Not just that, the last time we had sex, he was fighting hard not to bite me and claim me. He practically licked my skin off."

Carter blew out a long breath. "I don't know, Jesse. He's an Alpha, a wolf shifter, and the leader of the most prominent and powerful pack in the area. How would that even work?"

I dragged my hand through my hair and left it on the top of my head. "I'm worried about that for sure, but I'm more worried about hurting him. He's strong but naïve. I could break him."

"Then *you* need to decide what's best for him."

I released my hair and shook my head. "He's an Alpha. He'll decide what he wants."

"Then have a frank discussion with him. Warn him in a way he'll listen."

"I've already been blunt with him about my life. It didn't scare him off. He held me tighter and nuzzled the back of my head like I'd been talking about stubbing my toe."

"You need to get through to him. He's my boss, and I care about him."

Carter was right. I needed to talk to Lucas.

"I've got to shower before I head to his place."

"Scrub hard." Carter walked past me and opened a window.

Once home, after a reluctant partial hug from Carter, I washed my hair and body three times, even douched to ensure I smelled fresh and not like I'd fallen off the back of a garbage truck.

Many eyes were on me when I pulled up outside Lucas's cabin. A few wolf shifters walked toward me, their fangs erupting. I wasn't welcome here. I'm positive they could smell the lines of cocaine I'd done for courage before leaving. Drugs were strictly forbidden in Creekside Township.

The East Creekside wolf pack enforced that rule. The same pack that Lucas led.

What am I doing here?

I looked down at my wedding ring and took a deep breath. I'd sent Lucas a text saying I was back in town and wanted to see him. He'd suggested we meet at his cabin.

Lucas opened the front door as I mounted the steps.

His smile was genuine and warm. He was glad to see me. If he detected the cocaine on me, he didn't show it. I had a genuine battle not running to him to have him hold me again.

His pack gathered outside on the driveway wouldn't be impressed. I didn't want to embarrass him.

"Come on in," Lucas said and led me to the living room. I sat in a chair across from the sofa on which he had seated himself. I wasn't sure how close to be to him. Not until we talked first.

"Lucas, what happened about the annulment? Why the rings?"

Might as well dig right in.

"It's simple. I'm not ready to let you go."

"What if I walked away?"

"Then I would respect your decision."

Another concern poked away at my brain as I sat there staring at the immense wolf shifter who wanted to stay married to me. "What if my Alpha self doesn't want to do this the way we've been doing? What if I want to be in charge within our relationship?"

"Is that what you want?"

"I won't be your Omega, Lucas. We'll be equal, or this won't work."

"I wouldn't dream of having it any other way."

"You're in for hell with me ... you do understand that, right? The drugs, the drinking, the sex work, and not being coherent most of the time. You'll have to put up with all of that."

Lucas frowned at me but spoke what I knew was true in his heart.

"I'll be here for you, no matter what you throw at me."

I needed to make sure he completely understood what he was in for.

"I can't go a day without using, or I'll go into withdrawal."

"I know."

"I have to work to feed my addiction. I need to do the porn and dating."

Lucas's shoulders caved forward as if to protect his heart. And that was the part of him I was most worried about. He blinked at me and nodded, resigned to let me live my depraved life.

He had the most beautiful soul.

I blinked as tears gathered in my eyes. "I'm going to break your heart."

"My heart is stronger than you're giving me credit for."

"What about your pack? They're never going to accept me."

"Leave them to me. If I need to fight them for you, I will."

My heart sank. "You can't go changing your whole life for me like that."

"Jesse, you don't get it." Lucas shifted forward on the sofa. "I *want* this with you. I want you and everything you'll be bringing to the table as long as I can be with you."

Tears rolled down my cheeks. How had this incredible, sincere Alpha seen anything in me worth fighting for? I spun the ring on my finger. "I'll keep it on until you tell me to take it off."

"Is that a promise?"

I nodded, leaned forward, and clasped my hands together. "I promise." This was so far off from what I'd expected when I first woke up with Lucas after our wild night together.

For him to desire me, to need me, to want me ... it had never crossed my mind.

Married.

My mate.

Lucas dropped to his knees, made his way to me, and held me.

I don't remember the last time I'd cried as hard.

Chapter 7

LUCAS

I held Jesse tightly as his battered soul wept, gasping and crying, his shoulders jerking up and down as he fought for breath. My Alpha needed me, and I was here for him.

So many Alphas refused to cry or show their feelings. I sensed Jesse might have been distant like that when he was with Carter. Carter had told me Jesse had been his strong Alpha protector.

They'd been in love but not spoken the words.

It was such a sad story. Jesse had suffered. So had Carter. Yet, somehow, they had remained friends. Best friends. Carter saw in Jesse what I did—a tortured but wonderful creature.

Someone worth knowing.

Jesse clung to me, clutching my shirt and digging his fingers into my back. I pulled him to me, and he put his damp face against my neck and shuddered through the last of his tears.

When he pulled away, his face was crimson and puffy, and his nose was running. I snatched a tissue out of a box under the coffee table and handed it to him.

"Thank you." Jesse wiped his face and blew his nose. He kept the tissue bunched up in his hand. "Apparently, that needed to come out. I haven't cried in years."

"It's cleansing."

Jesse smiled at me. "So I've heard."

"Doesn't make you any less an Alpha."

Jesse nodded, and I continued because I was an idiot and wasn't prepared to listen to Maddox.

"What about rehab?" I asked.

He sniffed and sat back in his chair. I could smell the cocaine on his secretions.

"I need to phone them every day for ninety days to secure a spot. There's no way someone like me can do that. I disappear for days and emerge among time slips."

I'd spent some time reading about withdrawal on the internet. So, I had other ideas I wanted to run past Jesse. "What about getting on a methadone program?"

"It's hard to walk away from the high you get on real drugs. I tried methadone when we first moved here because of the drug ban in Creekside." He frowned. "I could try it again."

That's all I needed to hear—that he'd try. I brushed some of his dark blond hair behind his ear and moved closer to him. I wanted to kiss him, but he pressed on my chest and stopped me.

"Let's not go there. I want to, but let's see how this pans out without sex."

I gazed all over his striking and perfect face. "That's what you really want?"

"I think it's for the best right now. Especially if I'm going into recovery."

I nodded, and Jesse started talking about motorcycles. It was a quick subject change, but I had a love for them, too. We had lots to talk about. Bikes we'd ridden. Bikes we pined over. The best motocross riders we'd seen on television or in person at rallies.

We switched from that to our favorite movies and games. We both liked action crime-fighting films, and both had a penchant for *Zombie Wars*. I started up the game, and we spent the next three hours laughing and shouting at the television screen as we fought through a zombie apocalypse.

It was the laughing I liked best.

Jesse was so free and easy in this state. I turned a blind eye when he slipped a pill into his mouth. It didn't affect his gameplay, but I wondered what it was.

His world was so unfamiliar to me.

I needed to have a conversation with Maddox about him. Seeing me with Jesse, and it being obvious we'd been intimate, he must have questions. I'd been putting off phoning my brother.

Jesse wiped out the last zombie and won our latest game. He'd beat me 2-1. I set my controller on the coffee table and rose to my feet. "Do you want something to drink?"

He breathed hard a few times. "Just a glass of water, thanks."

"Coming right up."

I was fussing around in the kitchen, filling two glasses with water, when Jesse walked up behind me, wrapped his arms around my waist, and kissed the center of my back.

The embrace was an Alpha move. I'd promised him we would be equal in our statuses. I hummed and held his hands to my abs, and turned to face him when he directed me to.

Both of his hands went to my face, holding it, and he kissed me. It wasn't a sexual kiss. It was the kind of kiss mates shared when they felt particularly close.

I held him tightly as Jesse looked up at me.

"You undo me," he said.

I stroked his cheek and smiled. "Then my plan is working," echoing what he had said to me in the bathroom stall. He'd said it to be cheeky. I meant it. I planned to be his mate one day.

The smile he bestowed on me was stunning.

A brief kiss, and Jesse grabbed a glass of water and went back to the living room. I followed and sat beside him. After a few sips, he put his head on my shoulder and his hand on my thigh.

I covered his hand with mine.

"We're really doing this," I said.

"I'll do everything I can to make it work, I promise."

I knew Jesse meant it, but the pull of drugs was reportedly strong. Using them ripped entire families apart. People lost their jobs and ended up homeless after being homeowners.

Jesse stroked my hand with his fingers. "I really like you."

I smiled. "I really like you, too."

He glanced up at me. "Why?"

His question caught me off guard, but I had the answer.

"I can sense incredible strength beneath your addiction. I respect that. And I know you're capable of deep love and loyalty. Your friends have stood by you for a reason."

"I'm completely fucked up."

I took my hand from his and put my arm around his shoulders. I took a chance. We were cuddling. It was a safe space. "Do you mind telling me how it started?

Jesse sighed long and loud. "I took off when I was sixteen. My up-bringing came with demons that I'm trying to escape. Drugs, alcohol, and sex do that for me. Make me forget."

"How old are you now?"

"Twenty-six."

Ten years of homelessness and substance abuse. Jesse really *was* lucky to be alive. At nine years his senior, I hadn't experienced anything as distressing or dangerous in my life.

Was I too naïve for us to have a relationship?

"I don't want to hurt you," Jesse whispered.

"You let me worry about that."

"No, promise me, you'll ditch me if I become too much for you. Without explanation. If you can't do it anymore, leave. Don't let me drag you down. You mean too much to me."

I kissed his head. "I promise ... if it makes you feel better."

Jesse moved back, staring at me. "No, you have to mean it. Promise me."

How could I promise such a thing when I intended to fight for him? If it meant chaos mixed with moments of us being together, my heart was telling me I could handle it.

His expression was pleading with me.

"I promise."

After Jesse left, I decided to call my brother. It rang three times before he picked up. I knew he was probably at work, and I'd ignored his last piece of advice, but I wanted to update him to see if he had any more advice I might or might not heed, depending. He was my big brother. He'd been our pack leader for years. I needed his opinion.

"Hey, Lucas." He sounded cheery. Wedded bliss would do that for you, I guess. It was a stage that Jesse and I had missed out on. We'd gone straight from married to strife.

And confusion.

So much confusion, and my not knowing what the hell I was doing.

"I've been waiting for this call," he added. "What's happening with you and Jesse?"

"We got married the night of your stag party."

"You did what?"

"We were both drunk, and he was high on top of it. We ended up in bed together. Things must've become intense because we decided to hit up a wedding chapel."

"He's the one with the substance abuse you're worried about."

"Jesse is in pretty deep."

"Then why continue? You made a drunken mistake. Have it annulled."

"I tried that already. I couldn't do it. I couldn't sign the paper. I tore it up."

"Why? Do you have feelings for him?"

"He's so much more than his drug use. When he's sober, we really connect."

Maddox blew out a long breath. "Brother of mine, what have you got yourself into?"

"We've decided to try to make something of what we have together."

"Lucas ... he's a drug addict, and he's an Alpha bear shifter. What are you doing? The pack will never accept him as your mate or as your partner in leading the pack, you know that."

"Maybe I don't care."

"Of course, you care. Talk to our sire. Do that at least before you take what you and Jesse are doing any further. Promise me you'll talk to him, Lucas."

Our sire, Lucas Sr., would have something to say about what I was doing. How I was going against pack protocols. I'd already gotten an earful from my Beta, Clara.

My second promise of the day.

"I promise."

Two days later, I was with my sire, shifted to wolf form, and following the trail of a lame deer. Lucas Sr. didn't hunt much of late. He was nearly seventy, and his bones ached increasingly more each time he shifted. Plus, he had to work hard to keep up with our pack's pace.

They'd never leave him behind, which hampered their success, so he preferred to sit hunting out and only run with the pack for pleasure; to feel the breeze on his fur and immerse himself in the scent and sounds of the forest. To experience the freedom of being a wolf.

My primary purpose for being out here was to seek wisdom from the aging wolf. He'd seen a lot in his time with the pack as its leader. He'd always been open and accepting. Jesse and I weren't the first two male Alphas to pair up. My sire's own brother had both an Alpha *and* an Omega mate.

They'd produced an entire slew of pups over the years.

Jesse and I would never have that.

My sire jogged along beside me as we sniffed the trail. If we brought down the deer, it would be a bonus. His voice appeared in my mind through our wolf link.

"Why did you bring me out here?"

"I miss being shifted in the trees with you."

"There's something on your mind. What is it?"

"Maddox said I needed to talk to you."

Lucas Sr. snorted. *"And you decided to listen. Wonders never cease."*

"I got married last month."

Lucas Sr. stopped moving. *"I noticed the ring. Adam was pushing me to ask why you had it. I decided to let you tell me in your own time. Where is this mysterious Omega wolf?"*

"He's not an Omega."

"Adam suspected you might be with the same shifter you told him about." Lucas Sr. sat on his haunches. *"I'm not one to judge if he's an Alpha."*

"He is, but he's also a bear."

My sire's hackles went up. Jesse being a bear was a step too far.

"But you're the pack leader. You have appearances to maintain. Your mate needs to be a wolf at least. The pack looks up to you for guidance. This is unacceptable."

Even my liberal sire was coming out against Jesse and me.

"It's not going to change. I want Jesse in my life."

"Jesse! Carter and Rory's Jessie!"

"Don't yell at me."

"He lost his job with Creekside Motors because he was always high. Did you know that?"

"I'm not surprised, but we're working through it. He's seeking help."

"And you believe him? He's a drug addict. There's a reason we don't allow drugs in Creekside. They ruin people's lives. The drug addict and everyone around them."

"I trust him."

My sire huffed. *"You're delusional."*

I was breathing heavily, feeling distraught and misunderstood, when I took off into the woods at a speed Lucas Sr. couldn't match. He would find his own way home.

He didn't get it. My heart ached for time with Jesse. Whatever fleeting glimpses of his soul he'd be capable of giving me. And if he started treatment, there would be more of those moments.

I craved every word, every touch, every knowing glance.

I found the lame deer, but lost my footing while speeding toward her. However awkwardly, she took off into the trees, I didn't follow. I wanted to check my phone for messages from Jesse.

After running home, I opened his thread, and it made my heart sing.

"I miss you," were his words.

Me*: "I miss you, too."*

Jesse*: "Give me a few days to adjust to the methadone. Then I want to see you."*

Me*: "Sounds good."* I wanted to add more. How much he meant to me. *"Thinking of you."*

Jessie*: "Dreaming of your lips."*

Cheeky.

Me*: "Soon, my Jesse, soon."*

There was no reply. I wondered if my endearment had scared him. It was almost fifteen minutes later when he answered. *"I'm yours, Alpha."*

CHAPTER 8

JESSE

It didn't matter what game I played; I wasn't into it. I'd gone out this morning and taken my methadone at the pharmacy, then come home to find some way to entertain myself that didn't involve drugs or alcohol. Even my favorite *Zombie Wars* didn't hold my interest.

Maybe if Carter had been here playing it with me, the game would've been more fun. Or Lucas. We'd had a blast gaming at his cabin. Gaming and talking and laughing.

And making promises.

We had more in common than I'd been expecting.

I hadn't talked to him in a week, aside from a few text messages each day saying we missed one another or good night while lying in bed. I wanted to make sure I was well past the initial tiredness of starting methadone. What was left was the orneriness of living an everyday life.

I finished putting the last of the empty alcohol bottles into the recycling. Day one, I had dumped their contents down the kitchen sink. It had taken incredible conviction to do so.

Earlier today, I vacuumed, dusted, and washed the kitchen and bathroom floors. Carter had been stunned when I told him he didn't need to come by to do it for me; stunned and proud of me for trying to pull myself away from substance abuse.

Unfortunately, having a clear mind meant all my worst memories were now hanging around.

The reasons I had started alcohol and drugs in the first place.

I needed to deal with that, or I'd start using again. I fired off a quick text to Rory, asking for his therapist's name and contact information. He responded with it without asking questions.

I'd call on Monday if I felt brave enough.

I plopped down on the sofa and stared out the window to the trees beyond. I briefly thought about shifting and going for a run, as I'd started doing most afternoons, but decided to phone Lucas instead. It had been too long since I'd heard his voice.

He answered after the first ring.

"Hey, Jesse. How are you doing?"

"Feeling better. Stronger." In honesty, I was going out of my fucking mind. "I'm bored."

"Life isn't supposed to be exciting all the time."

"My life *was* exciting."

"Do you miss it?"

I had no problem being honest with Lucas. If this was going to work between us, there couldn't be any secrets. I had plans to tell him everything. "I miss all the fucking."

"Porn fucking?"

"Yup."

"Do you like doing porn?"

"I love it."

Lucas grunted. "I was hoping you were talking about us."

"I think we've moved past carnal fucking, you and I."

Lucas did a hmm. I wasn't sure if he was agreeing or not.

I hoped he was.

"Do you want to shift and meet in the woods by the rocky bend in the creek?" he asked. "Do you know which one I'm talking about?"

"I do." The thought of seeing Lucas made my heart patter wildly. "I'd love that." Then images crept in. The same images that had plagued me while shifting over the past couple of days.

Being sober meant they had free rein.

Somewhere around the age of twelve, my dad had introduced me to flogging as a form of contrition and punishment for wanting to shift. I had knelt on our cold basement floor every morning and used the biting leather strands on my back to remind me not to embrace my bear.

I'd wanted so desperately to please my parents.

Then one day, they searched my browser history—something they'd never done before, and they found the gay porn sites I'd been frequenting. I'd been forced to tell them I thought I was gay.

All hell had broken loose.

Lucas was everything my parents didn't want for me. Everything they tried to drive out of me. Everything they tried to control. Everything they came to hate about me.

The existence of a gay shifter in their family was abhorrent.

I remembered being blindfolded and hauled into the back of a vehicle in the middle of the night by strangers and brought somewhere where heinous nightmares were created.

I shifted and lumbered away from my cabin into the woods, and my mood lifted as Lucas came into view, a massive grey wolf whose presence almost triggered my flight response.

Only my feelings for him kept me from running away.

I lowered my head, and Lucas rubbed his snout on mine, sniffing and inhaling, imprinting my bear scent on his brain. I did the same.

He smelled like Lucas, but with an overtone of wet dog that would take a bit of getting used to. Lucas nudged me and set off at a lope into the trees.

We were going for distance at that speed. I wondered where he was taking me. What felt like an hour later, we emerged into a field of late summer berries. My hibernation instinct kicked in, and I set about gorging myself while Lucas nibbled berries off for himself beside me.

Before I was full, Lucas rumbled and barked, then took off at a run. I dug in and followed him. He was having an easier time weaving through the trees at top speed, whereas I crashed past them, snapping off lower branches and obliterating the odd bush.

Lucas came to a startling stop, his hackles went up, and he started growling. He lowered his body slightly, as if he was going to spring. It took my nose a few moments to catch up.

I could smell five of them: a small pack of wolves.

If I had to guess, they weren't from the East Creekside pack, and they had crossed into East Creekside territory. What they were doing here, I had no idea.

Once they were in front of us, one wolf from their pack stepped forward and shifted to human form. An Alpha. He was tall and muscular, and as ugly as the evergreen trees were green.

Lucas shifted, too, and approached him.

"What are you doing on our land?" Lucas asked.

"Chasing down an elk that started on ours."

"It crossed the boundary. It's no longer your elk."

The other wolf smirked. "Didn't expect to be found out so far north." Then he looked at me, his smirk turning into a sneer. "What are you doing running around with a bear?"

"We're friends out enjoying the forest."

He frowned. "You shouldn't be associating with bears. As leader, you know that."

"As leader, I also have a choice about who I hang around with. You should know *that*."

My hackles bristled. Was this interaction going to lead to a fight?

"I'm particularly friendly with his den of bears," Lucas said. "One of them works for me."

The Alpha wolf grunted. "You need to watch your step, Alpha. You should be running with your own kind. I'm sure your pack has the same take on this kind of indiscretion. Working with a bear is one thing. Practically frolicking in the woods with one is quite another."

Lucas stood tall and clenched his shoulder muscles until they were hard and powerful, and surged forward, challenging the wolf. "Head back across the boundary. And stay there."

He received a snort as a response. And without even the slightest bow to Lucas, the wolf shifted, and he and his pack turned and took off in the direction of their own territory.

The encounter made me feel uneasy.

West and East Creekside. I hadn't realized there was tension between the two packs.

I shifted so I could talk to Lucas. He perused my naked body without hesitation or shame. I was happy for him to do so. My cock thickened with each pass of his wandering gaze.

I completely forgot what I had planned on asking him.

Ever so slowly, Lucas crossed the forest floor to me and cupped my face. I melted against him as he kissed me. He only pulled away to whisper against my lips.

"I can't stop myself. My body and mind crave you and every moment I can have with you."

Then he stepped away, took my hand, and led me through the trees until we arrived in a small meadow. The sun shone down on it, intensifying the scent of the grasses within.

Lucas didn't stop until we reached the center, beneath a solitary deciduous tree. There he sat, encouraging me to do the same. I settled my ass between his legs, facing him, and encircled his waist with my thighs, my cock hardening further as I held his face and captured his mouth.

I wanted to climb inside him and never leave, breathing each breath in unison with his. I shifted closer until our stiff dicks met between us and crossed, Lucas's prodding my belly.

Undulating my hips to increase the tension, I clung tighter to his face and held him while I gasped, breathless, our lips barely touching. Lucas had promised we'd be equal partners.

"I want to fuck you," I whispered.

Lucas tensed, and the intensity of his exhalations increased. "I've never ...."

"You'll like it. I promise, I'll take care of you."

A slight nod accompanied Lucas's rapid breathing.

After untangling my legs from around his body, I placed my hands on his shoulders. He didn't resist when I pushed him over to lie on the grass on his back.

I found my place between his thighs and encouraged Lucas to bend his knees and let his legs fall open for me. I hummed with appreciation. His fat balls rested above the most perfect hairy crease. I vaguely recalled burying my face between them and feasting on his hole. I wished I could remember more of our first night together. I had no doubt it had been a touch deranged.

Maybe I'd even fucked him.

I leaned forward and licked the underside of his cock, then fondled his balls with my tongue, lathering, then sucking until he was thrusting his hips up. He went from that to growling when I took his dick into my mouth as I gripped the base—jacking and bobbing until he was at his limit.

I stopped, licked two fingers, and found his hole. He grunted, and his ring tightened when I touched it. I massaged and caressed until he relaxed. One finger pressed inside, I slid deeper. He was as slick as an Alpha could get. It was easy to add a second.

With the introduction of each new digit, Lucas's channel clamped down hard but then loosened. Four fingers later, he was moaning and swearing when I decided he was ready.

I knelt between his thighs and pushed them higher, tipping his ass up until I could see the full extent of what my prep had done. Lucas lifted his head and looked at me, his dark brown eyes, the same color as his chocolate-hued hair, exuding both apprehension and trust.

I lined up my cock and slowly advanced, not taking my attention off Lucas's expression, which exhibited some discomfort but wonder at the same time at what was happening.

Once I was balls deep, I took a moment.

"Are you all right?" I asked him.

"It burns, but I'm in awe of the fact you're inside me."

I tipped my ass back, vacating him slightly. He gripped my arms.

"Come back," he whispered.

I smiled down at him. "Hungry for more?"

Lucas licked his lips. "Yes."

I drew all the way back, then pressed forward, nice and high. Lucas whined, and his fingers dug into my forearms. He hung on as if I would leave him.

After setting a steady pace of thrusting and retreating, I pumped his cock, and Lucas bent his legs higher, hanging on to his knees and bringing them up to his underarms.

I took that as a sign to intensify what I was doing. The look on his face told me he'd reached that place of bliss and urgency. He wanted more. He wanted harder and faster.

I placed my hands on either side of his shoulders and thrust with a fervor that made Lucas groan and growl and fill the air with the sounds of pure, wonder-filled ecstasy.

His body clamped around my cock in rippling waves of pressure as he emptied his balls onto his stomach. I fucked every drop out of him, then roared to completion, filling his ass.

It felt like I'd bred him. Despite the difference in species, we'd mated. We'd been mating all along. This wasn't fucking. What we did together with our bodies meant more than that.

My breath ceased, held, depriving me, as I wove together what I was feeling.

Lucas had found his way into my heart.

I *loved* this wolf shifter.

But now wasn't the time to tell him. My emotions were too raw to open myself up like that; to engage in a conversation where he might not say it back. I needed to be sure he would.

I dumped myself beside him, sighing, and joined him in exhilarated laughter.

"That was ... wow," Lucas said, grinning. "I had no idea it would feel that good." He turned to face me. "That *you inside me* would feel that good."

"I told no lies."

Lucas smiled at me. "We didn't last long without having sex."

"It felt like forever."

I stretched my arms up over my head and chuckled when Lucas licked my underarm. He went from there across to my nipple, nipping and teasing. Then shifted closer and kissed me.

My nurturing side kicked in, and I wanted to hold him. To offer him protection and aftercare. He was hesitant, but with encouragement, he let me cradle him, his head on my chest. I ran my fingers up and down his arm to soothe him and kissed the top of his head.

"Are you feeling any regrets?" I asked.

Lucas chuckled. "Not at all."

"Good ... I'm here to talk if you need to." I waited until he fully relaxed. It was time for me to share with Lucas something that even Carter and Rory didn't know.

"I was an only child," I said.

Lucas smiled against my chest. "I was one of far too many."

I carded my fingers through his hair. "My family belonged to a group called *Children of Eleutheria*." Lucas lifted his head but didn't speak. He knew this wasn't an idle conversation I was embarking on. "More of a cult, really. Members took a vow not to shift to animal form."

Lucas frowned and set his head back on my chest.

"When I was eleven, my shift started happening spontaneously. My dad would bring me to the basement and punish me." Lucas started growling. I could feel the rumble vibrating inside me. "I believed them ... that shifting was bad and meant I was weak. I spent every morning in that basement flogging myself to remove the images of my shifted self from my mind."

Lucas raised his head again. There were tears in his eyes.

"You are *not* weak. You have incredible power within you."

My brow dipped for a moment, not fully agreeing with him. "Maybe."

Lucas propped himself on one arm so he could gaze down at me with his gorgeous eyes. He stroked my cheek. "Have you ever heard the name Charles Carter before?"

I shook my head. "No."

"He owns the cabin you're living in."

"Carter deals with our landlord. I don't know anything about him."

"You'll find this interesting. When Charles moved to Creekside, he told my sire that he was escaping from a cult that sounds identical to yours. He bought that cabin to live in and did so for over fifteen years. Recently, though, he was moved into a nursing home in Riverton."

I wrinkled my brow. "Then who has Carter been dealing with?"

"His daughter and her husband, Sandy and Carl Burman."

"And you think their Carter branch might be related to me?"

"I think there's a good chance. They share your last name, and your stories are very much the same. I can set up a meeting with them if you'd like."

A lump formed in my throat. I had a hell of a time getting it to release. The premise that I had family out here, only a short drive away in Riverton, caused a rush of anxiety.

I wasn't family-friendly material.

"Let me think about it for a while." If I were even going to consider meeting with them, it would have to wait. I was only one week into my recovery.

I looked like crap, and I was twitchy.

Lucas leaned down and gave me a swift kiss. "Whenever you're ready."

I brushed my fingers through his hair. "Is it all right if we stay out here forever?"

"I have a better idea. Come back to my cabin so I can ravish you properly."

Yum.

That sounded like a better idea than lying in the grass.

Rory had invited Carter and me over to his home for lunch and a chance to catch up. I hadn't seen either of them in ages. Carter hadn't been over to my home to tend to me in weeks. I hadn't been strung out, requiring him to be with me, and we hadn't had any quality time in months.

"Grab whatever you'd like out of the fridge," Rory said from out in the living room, where he was feeding Cleo. Watching her feed from him made my gut pull in all directions.

I hated the idea of jealousy ... but there it was.

Lucas and I hadn't had a conversation about cubs or pups, or whether we'd see them in our lives. It was too soon to bring it up. We hadn't even exchanged words of love yet.

I lifted a bubbly, grape-flavored water out of the fridge and went in search of a glass. Carter knew where he was going and lifted one down for me. I'd barely spent any time over at Rory's. I didn't like the way Denver looked at me with pity drawn all over his expression.

I was a grown bear-shifter. I made my own decisions. I didn't need anyone's pity. I needed their support as I tried to turn my life around. Carter and Rory gave me that.

Glass in hand, I sat on the sofa across from Rory and tried not to fixate on the sweet noises Cleo made as she fed. I raised my glass. "How long is she going to do that?"

Rory's brow furrowed. "Only another couple of minutes."

I shook my head. "No, I mean, when does she start eating real food?"

"We've started her on a meat mash mixed with my milk recently."

I wrinkled my nose.

Gross.

"Are you excited for her to shift?" I asked.

Rory smiled. "I can hardly wait to see what she looks like."

Carter stayed quiet, nursing his bubbly water. He and Rory had likely discussed these things between them already. They had a strong relationship that existed outside of me.

I didn't connect with either one of them enough. I needed to change that.

"What about you, Jesse?" Rory said. "How is the recovery going?"

I gripped my glass tighter. "It's been hard."

My gaze wandered to the furry and adorable cub in Rory's arms again. In the cult I'd grown up in, members were encouraged to adopt human babies. I was a rarity. Born before my parents decided that shifting was evil. I wondered if my mom ... *carrier* ever held me the way Rory held Cleo with love, devotion, and wanting the best for her offspring.

How had she gone from that to hating me?

Cleo made more cute cub noises.

No cubs or pups.

Carter and I could have had cubs together, but we had avoided mating when he was in heat to avoid bringing one into our living situation. A stray thought imagined all of us sitting here, both Rory and Carter nursing a cub. A cub that Carter and I had created because of our love for one another. A love that no longer existed. My only chance at cubs was gone.

"Lucas has given me the space I need to lay down a foundation of recovery. He's been amazing in his support of me." All good stuff, but had I made the right decision with Lucas?

"Sounds like he's going to be a good partner for you," Rory replied.

I shrugged. "We'll see."

"You're not sure?" Carter asked. "He talks about you all the time. He's proud of you."

Knowing that made my heart race, unsure about our future together. I loved the time I spent with Lucas. Craved and yearned for it. But then the doubt would inevitably creep in.

Why did Lucas want to hang around with the likes of me?

"He's brought out the best in you, I think," Rory said. "As my Alpha, I always knew you were in there. I used to look up to you ... still do in many ways. You're a powerhouse of strength."

I frowned. "How can you say that, Rory? I'm a drug addict."

"Maybe so, but you provided us with a warm and dry roof over our heads, plenty of good food, and protection from the evils of Metro City. I survived because of you."

Carter nodded. "I'm with Rory on this. You saved my ass from the path of destruction."

Their recollection sounded admirable, but I knew the truth. I'd been barely holding it together, caring for two Omegas. Making sure they were comfortable and safe. What I'd done wasn't commendable; it was strictly instinct. My Alpha self had been drawn to nurturing them.

I wondered what it would have been like if we'd formed a family unit. The owners of Creekside Motors, where I'd worked, were two Omega wolf shifters mated with one Alpha.

They'd found happiness.

I took a sip of my drink. "You give me too much credit. You were both the survivors."

Us being a throuple was a stupid image. I'd never loved Rory like that. And I would've made a terrible sire. I could barely manage my own life. Never mind that of a helpless cub.

Why the hell was Lucas still in my life?

He was a prominent pack leader. He could find his fated or chosen mate among any number of Omega wolf shifters who could give him pups. I was none of those things.

I shook my head as I looked down at the wood floors. I'd been on some fantasy ride, believing Lucas would be my mate one day. I was holding him back from finding happiness.

I loved him, but Lucas was too good for me.

I needed to let him go.

CHAPTER 9

LUCAS

I t had been a week since I heard from Jesse, and I was getting worried. He wasn't answering my text messages or calls, and he wasn't at his cabin—I'd checked for four nights straight.

And his motorcycle wasn't there.

Most worrying, Carter hadn't heard from him either, but he had a good idea where he was. That's why I was on my way to Metro City with a list of possible places Jesse might be if he'd relapsed—a homeless shelter, a street corner, and a few back alleys.

I clung tightly to my steering wheel.

Is this going to be my future with Jesse?

Endless relapses and trips to Metro City to pull him out of his old life?

I reminded myself that it's what I had taken on when I told Jesse I wanted to stay married. I had gone in with my eyes wide open as to how he might behave. And the chaos he might create.

My heart was all in.

Beating hard for him.

Two hours later, I stopped outside The Grand Metro, retrieved my overnight bag from the backseat, and handed my truck keys to the hotel's valet.

I'd packed for three days. I hoped that would be enough.

After checking in, I took a turn around the restaurant and bar to see if Jesse was there on a date. It was still early for that type of meeting. The lunch menu had only recently closed.

I ditched my bag in my room and then headed off. I checked the homeless shelter first, but they wouldn't share the names of the people staying there. I decided to pull someone aside who was hanging around out front. They knew Jesse but hadn't seen him, and told me to check the corner on the other side of the city that Carter had shared with me. I headed there next.

The only reprieve I got from the pouring rain was when I braved the subway system to get me there faster ... and drier. I went the wrong way, changed back to the correct direction, and after ten stops, followed the passengers getting off the subway like a sheep, hoping for the exit.

I emerged where my phone said I needed to be.

The street corner I was looking for was easy to spot. Milling around was a group of beautiful young males, dressed to advertise. Booty shorts and crop tops, showing off their wares.

But no Jesse.

I approached, and again, they knew Jesse but hadn't seen him since last night, which gave me hope. He *was* here in Metro City. Now I just needed to find him.

And then what?

Kidnap him against his will?

I had no idea what I was going to say to him or what I was going to do. I just knew I needed him back with me. I wanted him to fight against his darkness with me by his side.

My partner—my mate.

The alleyways Carter had told me about were close by, and I visited every one of them, even poking my head into temporary shelters to ask the inhabitants if they'd seen Jesse.

He'd spent two nights ago with one of them, after they had spotted Jesse tucked into a cold, wet doorway to sleep. I clutched my chest as he relayed the information.

My heart was bleeding.

I was sure of it.

My precious Jesse, out here in the harsh elements, turning tricks for his next fix.

The man in the shelter told me Jesse had talked about looking forward to a shower in a porn studio. But he didn't know which one he'd gone to.

Armed with that information, I went back to my hotel room, opened my laptop, and typed in *gay porn sites* into the browser. There were quite a few. I started with the first one located in the city. It had previews of the action for each of its porn stars on its website.

Jesse wasn't among them.

It wasn't until I searched the fourth site that I found him. He was secured to a table, his bottom half through an opening in a wall, his legs spread open and tied to that wall on the far side.

There was a lineup of males, all stroking their cocks as they waited for their turn. I couldn't look away. A robust male was pummeling Jesse, then the camera angle switched to Jesse's face.

His head was thrown back, his eyes closed, and he was moaning with pleasure. The camera switched back, and the male who had been fucking him finished. A close angle shot showed the cum leaking out of Jesse's ass, then the male using a Sharpie to make a line on the back of his thigh. It was a tally, and there were already six marks on his skin.

Skin I had touched and kissed. Skin that I didn't want to share with anyone else. I had to sit with what I'd seen for a few moments and force my surging anger into a rolling simmer.

He'd told me he loved doing porn. Now, I had seen it for myself.

I made note of the name of the porn studio and looked up their address. They were another subway ride away from the hotel to what I assumed would be a seedy neighborhood.

I wasn't wrong in my expectation. Even as a bear shifter, I kept glancing over my shoulder and looking at the pavement as I passed groups of males. I didn't want any trouble.

After miles of walking, tucked between two buildings covered in graffiti was a narrow doorway with a worse-for-wear painted sign that told me I had found my destination.

St. Sebastian Studios.

I tried the opaque glass door, but it was locked. A voice came out over an intercom.

"Can I help you?"

The security concern was warranted. This place was filled with males having sex with males. There were aggressive and homophobic groups that would have a problem with that.

I needed to think on my feet.

I used the term for the porn stars I had seen on the websites.

"I'd like to be a model."

"Step back for me so I can see you."

I took a step back and turned toward the intercom camera.

"You're a bit of a beast, aren't you? How tall are you?"

"Six-nine."

"Good lord. I'd love to see you in action. Are you alone?"

"Yes."

The door buzzed, and I yanked it open and looked at the decrepit and worn stairs leading to where I might find Jesse. At the top of the stairs sat a compact blond bombshell. He leapt from his seat behind a desk and slipped his arm through mine, and led me down a hallway.

"Maybe we could do a scene together," he said.

My cheeks warmed. "Sure ... yeah ... maybe."

"My name is Sunny, by the way. I'm not normally at the front desk."

"Lucas."

Sunny furrowed his brow. "Jet's Lucas?"

Jet?

Right, I had seen that at the beginning of Jesse's video teaser. They had introduced him as Jet.

"Yeah."

"He talks about you all the time." Sunny guided me into a large room with a sofa, a television, and a row of snack machines. "It's crazy that you two are married already."

How much had Jesse shared?

Sunny released me.

"Is he here?" I asked.

"Sure is, but he's filming a scene right now." Sunny smiled at me. "Wanna watch?"

My heart thudded, and my abs clenched.

Could I? Could I see him like that?

My urge to protect him from harm overpowered me. I needed to be near him. I nodded my head, and Sunny took me back out to the hallway and into another large room.

I entered behind a human male with a camera. There were males with cameras in two other areas of the room. One kept walking back and forth, crouched, focusing on something.

I stepped sideways so I could see.

Every molecule in my body felt like it started vibrating with fire.

Jesse was in the middle of a bed on all fours. He was accompanied by two senior, rotund-bellied, and hairy males. One with his cock in Jesse's ass. The other with his dick in Jesse's mouth.

My Jesse was coughing and making fake choking noises. I was substantial, and he'd never had any problem swallowing *my* cock. He slurped the dick to the end and dropped it from his mouth.

The whining and groaning sounds he started were familiar to me. I loved those sounds, but a stranger was invoking them. It should be me. Only me. Jesse was my Alpha mate.

The back of my neck burned as fur erupted, and my hackles went up.

My incisors descended.

Sunny made a squeak sound. Living in the city, he'd likely never seen a shifter shift before. My body felt like it had a volcano broiling in my gut, ready to erupt. I tried to control it, but the more I watched Jesse get fucked, the more volatile I became. I couldn't stand it any longer.

With a roar, I pushed past the camera in front of me and raced to the bed. Jesse registered shock when he saw me. He hadn't detected my scent; he'd been so immersed with the two males.

I grabbed his arm, hauled him off the mattress, and into the hallway.

"Lucas! What the hell?"

"I don't want you to be here."

Jesse yanked his arm away from my grasp. "Not really your choice, is it?"

I frowned at him. He wasn't acting like the Jesse I knew. "Why are you working?"

"Why do you think?" He placed his hands on his hips and then jerked his stiff cock. "This here." He shook his dick. "This here makes me enough money to feed my habit."

I took a couple of deep breaths. It was either that or I was going to throw up, or shift, or completely lose my mind. "What happened to the methadone?"

"There was no way to escape my past when I used it."

"But Jesse ...."

Jesse scowled. "I told you I was going to break your heart. You're living in a fantasy world if you think I'm going to give all this up. The drugs and the work that gets me those drugs."

I touched his shoulder. "Jesse ...."

He jerked away from me. "Stop it. I'm high as a fucking kite right now, and I'd like to stay that way for the rest of this scene. Those two guys are relentless."

The male who had been operating the camera in front of me charged into the hallway. "What the fuck is going on? You need to get back in there, Jet, and fluff those two gents back up so they can continue fucking you, or you're fired."

I wanted to punch the male in his angry, crimson face.

Jesse put his hand on my chest to stop me, which brought attention to the fact that I was growling. I slowed the ferocity and retracted my incisors. I wanted Jesse to come home with me.

He wouldn't do that if I went Alpha male on him.

"You need to leave," Jesse said.

"I'm not leaving without you."

"Yes, you are. And you're going to go home. I'm where I belong."

"No, you're not. You belong with me."

Jesse crossed his arms. "You're wrong."

How could he say that? We'd only started. We were on our way to something truly special. Tears gathered in my eyes. I was hurt and angry. My mind snapped. "Prove it. Take off your ring."

I wanted to know where we stood. Was this a break, or was this the end?

The presence of the ring on his finger meant that he wasn't done with me yet. I took a step back, my knees weak when Jesse took off his ring and pressed it to my chest.

"There. Now, go home."

Chapter 10

JESSE

I hit the wet pavement hard, and Darryl's car sped away, leaving me without a coat or shoes, and my pants and underwear around my ankles. And I didn't care. All I cared about was that Darryl had transferred $1500 into my bank account before pulling me into an empty warehouse.

He was still making me pay for ghosting him all those weeks ago. I touched my cheek. It was already swelling. So was my eye. And my jaw didn't feel like it was in the socket.

I knew I should go to the hospital. I'm sure I needed stitches after Darryl and his buddy beat the crap out of me in that cold, dark space with a leaking metal roof.

That was the deal. They'd beat me up, then *rape* me with their cocks, and the fat end of a baseball bat. Then dump me back onto the street miles from where they'd picked me up.

I lay there for a while, forcing air in and out within what I sensed were some broken ribs.

People walked past me, barely taking notice that I was injured and had my ass and cock out getting rained on with the rest of me. I tugged on the band of my underwear to at least cover my dick, then struggled and pushed myself up into a sitting position.

The pavement was freezing cold on my ass.

It felt good, soothing the ache. They'd battered my hole so severely, I'd blossomed more than once without meaning to, exposing my rose to the cold air.

Darryl and his buddy had loved it.

Called me a little slut and fucked it until they came.

Not sure how long we'd been there, but they'd recovered a few times, leaving me to sit on the wet cement floor while they grew their arousal in the comfort of Darryl's warm car.

We'd started the night with Darryl's buddy holding my hands behind my back, so Darryl could plow his fist into my face without me being able to protect myself.

He'd struck me until I saw stars and tasted blood. I could still taste it.

I licked my puffy lips.

We were scheduled to meet again on Friday night. I wasn't sure what he had planned for me. My ankles were still bruised and rope-burned from when he'd suspended me upside down in his basement last week. He'd stuck a lit candle in my hole and let it melt onto my delicate skin.

Cha-ching. Another $750.

Feeling like I could stand, I grabbed a fire hydrant and pulled myself and my pants up, and stumbled off down the nearest alley. It was late into the night, and I was exhausted.

I found a warm vent in the back doorway of a closed Italian restaurant and made myself as small and compact as possible to retain as much body heat as I could.

Thankfully, Darryl had left me with my trusty, leather satchel. I cooked a dose of heroin and injected it into the top of my foot. I felt instantly warmer.

Several hours later, I came to, and my body immediately warned me that I was too cold. I was shivering, and my bare feet were burning on the frigid pavement.

I closed my eyes and leaned my head against the metal door. The last proper bed I'd slept in was with Lucas after our romp in the meadow. I longed to be back in his bed with him.

I sucked in a shuddering breath.

No matter how hard I tried to stop, I kept loving Lucas desperately.

My abdomen clenched against the cold. I needed to get out of the elements and warm up. I decided to use some of my money to rent a room in a hotel that lets you pay by the hour.

I'd been there with johns more times than I could count.

When I reached the front door of the derelict hotel, I was so fatigued that I barely made it inside. Leaning heavily on the counter, I paid for six hours and registered under the name Jet.

A hot shower would feel good.

It was the first thing I did after locking myself in my room. I used the tiny bar of soap supplied to wash my hair and body. Not a great job, but better than I'd been.

After gingerly drying off, I wiped the condensation off the mirror and gave my face a proper look. I was unrecognizable. My skin was swollen and bruised, and I couldn't see well out of one eye. It was going to take weeks to heal the damage Darryl and his buddy had done.

A part of me, deep in my soul, wanted to call Lucas to rescue me. But I'd sold my phone for drug money. I'd even sold my beautiful motorcycle. It hurt, but not as much as withdrawal.

Besides, I was never going back to Creekside.

There's no way Lucas would want me now.

I collected my supplies and sat in the middle of the bed, cooking. Even in my feet, it was becoming difficult to find a vein. I decided to find one in my groin instead.

Hours later, after lapsing in and out of consciousness, I emerged when someone hammered on my door. I scowled as I rolled over. They hammered again, but I just wanted to sleep.

"Fuck off!"

"Jesse!"

Oh, come on.

How had Lucas found me?

Carter.

Carter knew I frequented this hotel. So had he when he was down here with me working. It would've been easy for the front desk attendant to sell me out for a healthy cash payment if I'd shown up here under the name Jesse or Jet. They'd been sly in tracking me down.

"Go away!"

I jumped when something heavy smashed into the door. Then hit it again.

Jeezus, fuck ... he's breaking down the door.

The next blast, and the wooden door and frame splintered, and Lucas burst into the room. He slowed as he looked at the hideous state of my bruised and beaten face and body.

He clenched his fists. "Who did this to you?"

"Doesn't matter. He paid me to do it."

Lucas's brow furrowed hard. "You let someone beat you up for money?"

"$1500. It's good money."

Lucas growled, and the rumbling escalated. "You need medical attention."

"Absolutely not."

"Then I'm taking you home to tend to you."

I shook my head. "Lucas ... please go. Leave me here. I *want* to be here."

"Bullshit. You belong with *me*."

I glared at Lucas. "Give me one good reason to go with you other than I belong with you."

Lucas took three quick breaths.

"How about I'm in love with you? Is that good enough?"

I gripped the bedding.

How?

I covered my mouth with my hand as tears gathered until my limited sight turned blurry. How had someone as pure and good as Lucas fallen in love with *me*?

Lucas came to the bedside and kneeled beside me. I couldn't stop myself from cradling his kind, patient, and accepting face—his loving gaze fixed on me.

He loved me.

Lucas Black loved *me*.

I swept my drug paraphernalia aside, shuffled closer to him, and carded my fingers through his hair. Now was the time, if there was ever going to be one.

"I love you, too," I whispered.

He heard me because he broke down. I stroked his hair as he cried, face down on the bedding. I never wanted to be apart from him again. The revealing of our shared love had brought him to tears. Relief but also distress. He had no idea what was going to happen next with me.

I lifted his face until I could see his reddened, glassy eyes.

And put him out of his misery.

"I'm ready. Get me out of here."

Lucas's shower felt better than the shower at the hotel in Metro City. It was hotter, and it had deliciously earthy shampoo and soap he'd told me were cedar and rosemary scented.

He'd offered to come in with me, but I needed more alone time. He'd agreed to keep away from the shower, and his need to wash me, in exchange for my letting him patch me up.

As I dried myself, I looked at the pair of boxer shorts Lucas had set on the bathroom counter for me. They were flannel and looked cozy—and they were his. I slipped them on, along with a t-shirt, and went down to the kitchen, the agreed-upon location for Lucas to play doctor with me.

I stopped in the doorway. Lucas was wrapping up what sounded like a heated argument with a greying, female wolf shifter. His final word was that I was staying here.

She glared at me, taken aback by my appearance for a mere second. Her glare turned into a scowl, and she huffed out a grunt and shoved past me. The front door slammed.

I wandered into the kitchen, feeling like I shouldn't be there.

I should be back at my cabin.

I was causing problems for Lucas.

"Who was that?"

"That's Clara. My Beta. The wolf that picks up the slack for me and keeps me informed of pack dynamics. And right now, she is *not* happy with your presence in my home."

"What did you tell her?"

Lucas smiled at me. "That you're my mate and I love you." He stuck his hand in his pocket. "Which reminds me." When he withdrew his hand, he was holding my wedding ring. I'd stared at the wedding ring on *his* finger all the way home from Metro City as he drove.

After everything I'd put him through, Lucas hadn't taken his off.

He held up mine. "I want this to mean something this time when I put it on you."

I placed my hand over my heart. "Love?"

"Yes, exactly that. I love you, and you've said you love me, too. Can we agree on that?"

I breathed in and out, deep and long, relaxing. There was nowhere I'd rather be than with this incredible wolf. I walked to him, buried my face against his chest, and hugged him.

Chapter 11

LUCAS

Jesse had locked me in an embrace I never wanted to leave, but he hadn't responded to me. If I put this wedding ring back on his finger, it needed to mean something this time.

I knew he loved me, but I needed action.

I needed to know he wanted to be my mate.

Jesse moved his hands from my back onto my shoulders as he stepped back. My eyebrows peaked in surprise when he went down on one knee, and motioned for me to do the same.

I immediately liked this idea.

"Take your ring off," he said with his hand outstretched, and waited for me to hand it to him. He held it, raised it to his lips, and kissed it. "This is my promise to you." He peered at me with his one good eye. "I will come to you first if I'm struggling. And I expect you to do the same. I will be with you by your side as your mate through whatever life throws at us. I will always endeavour to put you first. And most of all, I will love you with as much as my heart is able."

His words filled my heart to overflowing.

Love was too simple a word for what I felt for Jesse.

I extended my left hand, and Jesse slipped my ring back on.

I held up his ring and kissed it. "This is my promise to you. I will come to you if I am struggling and will include you in all aspects of my life. You will be my mate and my partner. I will embrace and cherish your willingness to be by my side in my crazy, busy life." I smiled at him. "And most of all, I will love you through it all for as long as my heart is beating."

Jesse's hand shook as I placed his ring back on it.

Where it belonged.

Tears ran in slow rivulets down Jesse's cheeks. "Do you mean that? For life?"

I stroked some hair away from his cheek. His eyebrow was split and open. "Yes, for life. You have the warmest and most courageous heart I have ever imagined falling in love with."

Jesse licked his bruised and swollen lips. "Then I'll spend an eternity caring for yours."

We both chuckled a little at how sappy we'd become, but this was important. All the words we had spoken needed to be said. We needed to commit ourselves to one another.

I helped Jesse to his feet and urged him to sit on a stool at the island, and opened the industrial first-aid kit I'd pulled from my truck. Jesse had done a great job washing the blood off his skin, but there were a few repairs to do. The worst was through his eyebrow. I was going to need to debride the edges if it was going to heal without a thick scar. I wasn't sure Jesse would be into that.

It certainly couldn't be worse than how he'd ended up like this in the first place.

I touched the split skin. "I'm going to have to cut some of the dead tissue away from here."

Jesse tensed. "Do what you have to do."

"I wish I had some way to lessen the pain." I immediately caught what I had said. The last thing I wanted to do was suggest or encourage him to take opioids.

"Don't need it." Jesse grasped my belt. "Just do it."

I focused but was on the verge of cringing as I lifted each side with tweezers and cut away the dead skin. Jessie didn't move. His cut was much healthier looking when I finished.

He blinked his one good eye. "I was in prison for twelve and a half months."

I chuckled. "Were you really. Can't say I'm surprised."

Jessie smacked my arm, smiling. "Fuck off."

"What were you in for?" I arranged the supplies I'd need next.

"Theft and robbery."

"Was it lucrative at least?"

"Very. Helped us get enough money together to move to Creek-side."

"Then I'm not mad." I tipped his head back. "Now, hold still."

Jessie gripped my belt tighter, wrenching me forward as I stitched the wound closed. The rest of his cuts just needed glue and a prayer. There was nothing I could do about his split lip.

I held his face in one hand and turned his head back and forth. "I'd like to say you look better, but that would be a lie. You look like I've created my own version of Frankenstein."

Jesse laughed.

It sounded like heaven.

I looked out at the night sky through the kitchen window. "We should get some sleep."

Jesse nodded. "Long agonizing day."

"Do you need to talk about it?"

"Not tonight. Tonight, I need you to hold me." He slipped off the stool, took my hand, and led me upstairs to my bedroom ... *our* bedroom. This was Jesse's home now.

I was gentle with Jesse as I held him in bed. He suspected he had a few broken ribs, but noticed no signs that his lungs were having any trouble. With reluctance, I decided to trust him and fell asleep to the sound of his soft breathing and comforting scent.

When I woke, it was morning, and Jesse was pacing back and forth across the bedroom. He rushed to the end of the bed when he caught me looking at him.

"Oh, good, you're awake."

"Did you sleep?"

"A bit." He wrapped his arms around his stomach. "You need to get up. We have to go to the walk-in clinic before it gets too busy. I need my methadone."

Right.

He must be hurting already.

I swung my legs out of bed. "Let me get dressed, and we'll go."

Jesse looked down at himself. "What am I going to wear? My clothes have blood on them. And I can't exactly wear pajamas in public. I mean, I could ... but I don't want to."

I walked over to the dresser. "You can borrow something of mine." Thankfully, it was still warm enough to wear shorts, which were the only bottoms I had that would fit him because of our height difference. I handed him a pair and a sweatshirt. It was early enough in the day to be chilly.

Jesse took them from me and undressed. Whoever had beaten him up had really worked him over. What kind of sick fuck pays to beat someone up? Had they had sex with him after?

"Who did that to you?"

"Guess." Jesse pulled on the shorts without underwear.

"The same prick I saw you having dinner with?"

Jesse nodded, and my hackles pressed against my skin.

"I ghosted him, and I had some punishment to go through before we got back on track with our regular dates."

A rumbling growl built in my chest.

I was going to torture, then kill him.

Jesse pulled on the sweatshirt, stepped close, and put his hand on my chest.

"Slow it down, Alpha. I agreed to it. I didn't have to do it."

I felt sick. "Don't tell me you enjoyed it."

"No, that was a bit much for me. I'm all for being degraded, but normally I would draw the line at long, painful suffering. Make me crawl down the street naked with a collar and ball gag, all over it. Hang me up. Strap me. Relieve yourself on my face. I love the whole damned thing."

Fuck.

Tears rimmed my eyes. I brushed my hand through his hair.

"I can't give you any of that."

Jesse shook his head. "No, I don't want you to do any of that to me. That was my old life. What you and I have together is so much better."

Then why?

"The degradation ... were you trying to punish yourself for wanting to shift?"

Jesse blew out a gust of breath. "Maybe? Something I need to work through in therapy."

This was a new development. "You're in therapy?"

"As soon as I make the initial phone call. Rory gave me the contact info for his therapist."

I pulled Jesse into my arms and hugged him. "I think that's an amazing first step."

Jesse only let me hold him for a few seconds. He was squirmy. He wanted to get going so he could get his prescription into him. Once he was level-headed on the methadone, I'd let him borrow my truck to get his daily dose. I trusted him, and I wanted him to be independent.

Jesse tapped his fingers on the armrest of my truck all the way into town. While we were in the walk-in clinic waiting room, he wrapped his arms around his stomach, bent forward, and put his head on his knees. Everyone around us looked at him. He was obviously going through something. I rubbed Jesse's back until he was called in to see a doctor.

Standing, he found my hand and pulled me along with him. I felt incredibly honored and even closer to him, knowing he wanted me to come in to see the doctor with him.

More sitting and waiting once we got into a room, I kept checking the time on my phone. I sent Carter a text to see if he was okay at the job site on his own. Told him why I was skipping out. He had questions I didn't answer and would leave for another time.

I wasn't in the mood to explain what Jesse and I had shared with our words of commitment. That was between us for the time being. Carter would find out soon enough.

Almost fifteen minutes later, the door opened, and a man in expensive, casual clothes walked in. He looked to be Jesse's age. It felt like doctors kept getting younger.

"Jesse Carter?"

Jesse lifted his head and nodded. Sitting on the examining bed, he'd been bent over his legs again. I wished I could take away the intense discomfort he was going through and shoulder it.

"I'm Dr. Sudi. We've seen each other before."

Jesse licked his lips. "Yeah, I know. I remember."

The doctor perused Jesse's facial injuries. "What happened to you?"

"I was in Metro City ... got beaten up and robbed."

Dr. Sudi sat on a stool. "Did you visit the emergency room?"

Jesse shook his head. "Managed on my own."

"When did this happen?'

"Yesterday, but I'm all right."

"Did you lose consciousness?"

"Definitely not. Wish I had."

"Were you confused afterward?"

"For a few hours, I had trouble thinking straight."

"And now?"

"I'm all good."

"Was your torso involved?"

"Yeah, I got kicked a few times."

The doctor stood. "Can you lift your sweatshirt so I can check you over?"

Jesse grunted but did as instructed. Dr. Sudi felt his bruised ribs with his fingers, likely taking note of the fact that Jesse was wincing. "Can I get you to lie down, please?"

My mate was hesitant, but he eventually lay down. The doctor palpated his belly. "Does any of this hurt?" Jesse shook his head. Dr. Sudi seemed satisfied. He patted Jesse on the shoulder and supported him as he sat. "You're reasonably good. What else can I help you with?"

"Methadone."

"A new prescription?"

"Yeah, I fell off the sobriety wagon. Climbing back on for good this time."

"When was the last time you used?"

"Yesterday. Heroin."

The doctor started writing on a prescription pad. "Starting you on a mid-dose because you tolerated it well to start last time. We'll increase it as needed. I want you back in a week."

"I can do that."

Dr. Sudi looked at me. "And who's this with you?"

Jesse managed a sweet smile as he gazed over at me. "Lucas. My husband."

The doctor frowned, then handed Jesse the prescription. "This is only for a week." Dr. Sudi knew exactly who I was, and it was likely on Jesse's chart that he was a bear shifter.

Even as a human, Dr. Sudi seemed to have issues with mixed-species relationships. Carter had told me what he and Shaun had been through. How they'd been on the receiving end of much prejudice, hatred, and rejection. Jesse and I had that coming our way, too.

"We'll make an appointment on our way out," I said and growled, exerting my authority over him. Whatever position he thought he held in the community, ultimately, I was in charge.

Creekside Township belonged to the East Creekside wolf pack. The humans were allowed to live and work here because my pack granted them permission to do so.

Sometimes they needed to be reminded of that.

Jesse clutched my arm as we headed back to the waiting room. I made the appointment and put the date and time in my phone. I'd come with him again if he wanted me to.

That's what mates did; they supported one another.

The next stop was the pharmacy. Jesse dashed in ahead of me. When I caught up with him, he was already at the drop-off counter, handing in the prescription.

Then more waiting. Jesse was getting twitchy.

He leapt from the seat where he'd been perched and approached the counter when they called his name. The pharmacist set a small paper cup in front of him.

Jesse downed the contents in one shot.

A few sips of water after that, and we were done with that part of our day.

I started the drive to Jesse's cabin. He was much calmer now. So much so that he nodded off, his head leaning against the window. I didn't rouse him until we'd arrived at his place.

Jesse blinked his eyes open and sat up when I touched him.

"I thought it might be a good idea for you to grab some clothes and personal stuff."

Jesse turned to face me. "Am I moving in with you?"

My eyebrows raised without any instruction from me. "We shared vows. I assumed that meant you were going to be my mate and live with me."

Jesse furrowed his brow. "Yeah, of course ... it just happened so fast."

"Too fast? I don't want to pressure you."

He reached for my hand and clung to it. "No, it's the perfect speed."

Thank God.

Not sure I could drop Jesse off here and go home alone. He squeezed my hand, then got out of the truck. I followed him into the cabin in case he needed help carrying anything.

I was shocked by the state of his closet. He had very few clothes. They hadn't been a priority for him. Some of the clothes were wholly inappropriate and looked like the outfits I'd seen the young males on the corner of Metro City wearing. He collected the other options, handed everything to me, and went over to his dresser. The situation in there wasn't any better.

"I don't have much," he said. "I'll buy some clothes with the money I have left."

I'm glad he'd said that, because I hadn't wanted to step on his toes by offering to buy him clothes. Jesse was an Alpha. He would want to take care of himself.

"These will do you for now," I said. "You can always borrow from me."

"And look like I'm drowning in my clothes ... no thanks." Jesse smiled at me. He was feeling better than how I'd found him this morning. He yawned wide enough to swallow the sun.

He'd told me the methadone would make him sleepy for a while until he was used to his maintenance dose. I needed to get him home. He grabbed a few things out of the bathroom.

When we arrived at *our* cabin, Jesse went straight upstairs and lay down. I followed while texting Carter to let him know I was taking a few days off. He could handle any tasks that needed to be completed on his own. Carter had more questions that I ignored for now.

I wanted to spend time with Jesse.

This wasn't much of a honeymoon, but it would have to do for now.

Jesse sighed and looked at the ceiling as I settled in beside him. "I just realized ... I don't have my phone anymore. Could you ask Carter to get Rory's therapist's contact information for me again? I want to make an appointment with them for this week if possible."

I turned and kissed his cheek. "Proud of you."

"I'm determined to make this work between us."

"I have faith in you."

Jesse wrinkled his nose. "Faith. That was used as a weapon against me."

I raised myself on one elbow so I could look down at my mate. "How?"

Jesse rolled his eyes and sighed. "My parents found out I was gay, and that didn't align with what they were trying to mold me into. An obedient, pious, family man."

"Man?"

"We didn't use the term *male* in my household. That was considered shifter language."

I brushed the back of my fingers down his cheek. "Go back to *faith*."

Jesse hesitated. "They dragged me off in the middle of the night, blindfolded and with my arms tied behind my back. Threw me in the back of what I assume was a van."

"Who did?"

Jesse closed his eyes, vacated ... then startled to sudden consciousness.

By some miracle, he remembered my question.

"The goons for the conversion therapy camp my parents signed me up for."

"Jeezus."

"I wish. I would've appreciated him being there as they tried to dismantle me and put me back together in a form they and my parents found pleasing."

"As in, not gay."

Jesse laughed with a strained sounding voice. "The methods they used weren't much worse than what my dad was already putting me through. My favorite, though, was them showing me images of naked men and delivering a shock through electrodes on my fingers with each one."

He closed his eyes and stroked my arm.

I waited through his many breaths until he spoke again.

"All it did was develop an association between gay sex and discomfort within me. One that I grew to like. When they saw I kept getting erections, they switched tactics. Locked me in a pitch-black room with a hard bed, no pillow, and a bucket for a toilet, and starved me. The only sound was the blasting of Bible scripture against men lying with men, and the gospels on repeat."

What the hell?

"By day four, with nothing but water passed through an opening in the door, I felt like I was losing my grip on reality. I started having nightmares that turned into day terrors.

"I saw all sorts of creatures around me. By day seven, I was convinced I was dying. That's when they let me out. Let me eat a meal, then threw me back in the room."

I lay back beside him and buried my face against his arm so that I wouldn't cry out. He'd been through so much. Life-altering events for which I had no frame of reference.

"I lost so much weight, I was unrecognizable by the time they finished two more rotations. Ghastly pale with sunken eyes and prominent cheeks. I had trouble walking. I crawled out of there. This time, when they showed me the male nudes, my body was too exhausted to respond."

Jesse sighed.

"They thought they'd cured me."

A growl threatened to erupt. "Cured you of preferring males. That's ludicrous." I rolled back slightly so I could see his face again. The bruises were turning new colors of purple.

He was silent for a few moments, then Jesse entwined his fingers with mine and peered along his shoulder at me. "What about you?"

"What about me?"

"Do you prefer males?"

"I do, but I have enough interest in females, I could've made a mating situation work."

Jesse wrinkled his nose. "Nope. Not me."

"A female never tried to hire you as an escort?"

"Plenty, but I turned them down."

I tipped my head to touch Jesse's. "Do you think you were left with mental scars?"

"From the conversion crap? Absolutely. The top two things on my list for therapy. Shifting denial and praying away the gay. I think the way the rest of my life unfolded stems from both."

"Is that why you left your home so young?"

Jesse squeezed my hand. "My parents caught me with a male in my bedroom. Doing *stuff*. They were going to send me back to conversion camp. I shifted into a bear the night the goons showed up. I had a lot of repressed aggression from containing my inner self."

He shrugged. "May have been some injuries."

"You went Alpha bear on the captors?"

"Fucked them up, then took off running."

"Where did you go?"

"I was nude from shifting, so I hit up the homeless shelter downtown. They dressed and fed me and gave me a bed for a few nights. Sitting bored out front one day, someone introduced me to fentanyl. Being numb like that gave me an escape I hadn't known existed. I was hooked.

"Spent the next 5 years surviving. I gained some respect on the streets. Had my shelter with all the amenities, and plenty of food. I used to dumpster dive behind all the best delicatessens, plus steal stuff from stores and resell it. I was doing well, keeping myself alive, and my addiction fed.

"Then Carter came into my life, and everything was flipped on its head. I fell in love with him from the first moment I set eyes on him. He was the Omega to my Alpha."

"Fated?"

"That's more of a wolf thing. More like we were destined to meet."

"You used to run as bears together."

Jesse laughed. "In Central Park, late at night. Scary as hell. There were security guards with guns in there for their protection. They definitely would have shot us."

"The shift felt good?"

"The first time we did it was to find out if Carter's injuries would lessen in bear form. I hadn't shifted since I attacked those human males trying to kidnap me. But I did for him."

"Because you loved him."

"To the depth of my soul. After the first time we shifted, it became easier, and I started to enjoy it. Even craved it. I felt more alive while in bear form. Most of the time."

"Do you still have hangups about shifting?"

"The punishment ... for doing it ... is etched in ... my skin. I'll never be ... completely free."

His words had come out slurred and quiet—almost a whisper. I sensed I'd lose him soon. I didn't want to keep him from the sleep he needed.

"I hope the therapist gives you some tools to work through that." Which reminded me. I took out my phone and texted Carter to ask Rory for the contact information Jesse needed.

Jesse closed his eyes, and his breathing slowed.

He hummed when I kissed his forehead.

I'd let him sleep for as long as he needed. Make some lunch in a couple of hours in case he woke. If not, dinner would be ready as well. I'd keep him fed and comfortable.

I spent my afternoon in the office, catching up on bookkeeping stuff for Black Electric and the pack finances. Every member of the pack was required to pay me a percentage of their income to meet the pack's needs as a single entity. The construction of new dwellings, land maintenance, and the provision of personal loans for items such as work equipment and/or vehicles.

I knew enough about Jesse to realize that he was a strong Alpha and would want to become integral in the pack's workings. To lead by my side. He wouldn't be satisfied with make-work projects. His role would see him taking on some of Clara's tasks and making important pack decisions with me. He would truly be my mate and partner in every way.

But for now, Jesse needed to rest and recover.

CHAPTER 12

JESSE

I opened my eyes to a feeling I hadn't had in a very long time. My state of being felt as *normal* as it had been before I took off for the streets and used drugs for the first time.

I lay there looking up at the ceiling, then over to my right. Lucas was fast asleep, with a gentle snore that helped lull me to sleep each night. I'd been living with my mate for a month now.

Couldn't honestly be happier.

I owed most of that to Lucas and his patience with me, and part of it to the progress I was making in therapy, dealing with my residual shame around shifting and substance abuse.

I stretched my arms and legs. It all felt fantastic. I dismissed an early morning thought that still plagued me to get up and go in search of my next fix. I fought hard every day.

This morning felt different, though. The urge had lessened. I was more focused on the sleeping form of my gorgeous mate. We hadn't been intimate since before I took off to Metro City. I hadn't felt like it, and Lucas was vehement about letting me heal, body and mind first.

My cock stirred the more I watched him. I wanted to do sinful things to him, and smiled as I slipped beneath the covers, all the way down to the bottom and over, between his legs.

His dick was semi-hard and resting on his fat, delicious balls. *I might visit those later.* Instead, I took his shaft in my hand, licked the underside, and capped his cockhead with my lips.

Lucas stirred but didn't wake.

I squirmed against the sheet, jamming my hardening cock against it, then took Lucas's dick into my mouth and sucked and bobbed on it. He kept shifting his ass, then he placed his hand on my head and grasped my hair, groaning. He'd awoken to my impromptu sexy surprise.

Lucas didn't say a word as I pumped and slurped on his dick until he came in my mouth. Only a shuddering whine as I swallowed every delicious drop and left him as clean as when I started.

He touched my shoulder, and I crawled up his body and shared the taste of his seed with him by kissing him and reveling in his exploring my mouth. I jammed my knee against the mattress beside his inner thigh and put pressure on it. He moved it aside and rolled his hips up.

I reached down and slipped a finger inside him, then two, and scissored him open.

"Please," Lucas whispered. "I'm ready."

I loved that those were his first words this morning. I slipped my fingers from his ass, gripped my hard dick, and pressed it to his hole. He grasped me around the waist.

I moved my arms to either side of him for support and slid my cock in slowly until it was home, where it *should* be every single day. I retreated, and Lucas whimpered and moved his hands to my ass, tugging me forward, wanting me back. I obliged and thrust up into him.

Focusing on his lips and eyes, I started a perfectly rhythmic and gentle assault on his ass. Lucas groaned and gasped and clung to my flesh wherever he could find to hold on.

His eyes were like two decadent chocolate pools amongst snow as he looked up at me. And they were both beseeching me and exhibiting divine pleasure. I'd opened Lucas's world, and he was thoroughly reveling in it. And for me, it felt good to be an Alpha lover.

I captured his mouth, showing him with my lips how much I loved him. I moved from the comfort of them to his ear, teasing and sucking his lobe, then down his neck.

When I arrived halfway to his shoulder, my incisors burned to erupt, so I let them. I dragged them back and forth across his skin. Lucas whined and squirmed and clung tighter to me.

"Do it," he bellowed with an urgency I hadn't heard from him before.

I licked what I knew was a wolf's claiming area, and pressed the points of my incisors against his flesh. Mine were significantly thicker than a wolf's.

I was going to hurt him if I followed through.

Lucas gripped me tighter. "Do it." Even louder. "Make me your forever mate."

I inhaled the scent of him. It had changed from arousal to something spicier, plus, I swear I could smell the blood that flowed beneath my lips. I pumped my hips harder and faster.

I wanted to cum while I was doing this.

So close. I battered his hole and grew frantic. My whole body was vibrating, wanting to taste the very essence of him. I couldn't stop myself if I tried.

I jerked my hips forward, filling him.

And bit into him.

He yelled, surrounding us with sounds of agony. It didn't stop me from biting down fully and getting my first taste of his blood. He clamped his hand onto the back of my head and held me in place while I sucked and swallowed, repeatedly, thrilling my very being.

As I suckled on him, a rush of clarity and insight filled my mind. I could feel his love for me, as if I were gathering it from within him. I felt other things, too. Total bliss and fulfillment.

The thoughts weren't mine.

I released his flesh and looked down at him, my incisors dripping blood onto his throat.

"I felt it, too," he said. "We've linked. Not as strong as a wolf would have done, but our minds linked. I could sense what you were feeling." He smiled at me. "Your love feels good."

I licked my lips, then retracted my incisors. "Yours washed over me."

Lucas wrapped his arms around my body and rolled me until I was under him.

He grinned at me. "My turn."

I dug my fingers into his hair and brought him down to my mouth. Once again, I shared the taste of Lucas with him as he prodded my balls with his thick, firm cock.

Opening my legs wider for him, he lifted them onto his shoulders and pierced me hard and high. He wanted to claim me in more ways than one this morning.

I was his, and he was going to let me know it.

Lucas grunted in my ear with each heavy thrust of his hips, pummeling me into the sheets. His aggressive fervor was glorious. I linked my ankles behind his back, sealing us together.

I closed my eyes and arched my spine, making substantial huffing noises like I was about to charge through the forest after a scent of prey. We were two Alphas locked to one another.

I gripped him around the back of his neck when I felt his cock thicken at the base, stretching me wider. I'd heard this about wolves, but it had never happened between us before.

With incredible force, Lucas jammed the knot inside me and froze. As the first of the warmth flooded me, he licked my claiming area, then clamped down, piercing me with his incisors.

My body and voice screamed with pain, but it soon subsided as he drank from me, his hips pumping as his cum coated my guts. Euphoria enveloped me, and I felt like I was floating.

So much better than any drug I had ever taken.

A tweak of unfamiliar consciousness flowed again. Lucas said we'd formed a link—a weak one, but one, nonetheless. I spent a moment peering into him.

Behind the love, bliss, and fulfillment was concern.

For me.

A growl started deep in Lucas's chest, then he unlatched from me, raised his head, and howled the most beautiful song I'd ever heard. In the distance, I could hear the howl of one other.

I knew there should have been more. Lucas had claimed me and wanted everyone in his pack to know. The entire pack should have responded to our status as claimed mates.

To assure him of my unending devotion in contrast to the lack of support from his pack, I gathered the feelings of hope and wonder I'd been having and pushed them his way, then grabbed his head and kissed his bloody lips. I could tell when he received it, because he kissed me harder.

A connection like this would take some getting used to.

And I wasn't entirely ready.

I pictured shutters in my mind and closed it off. I didn't want Lucas to see the struggles I was still having with my addictions and how they ran rampant most days.

They weren't as strong, but they were still there.

My mate didn't object.

Lucas tumbled onto the bed beside me and, with his fingers, felt where I had bitten him. "That's going to take a while to heal. You have some seriously thick incisors."

"It'll bruise big time, I think." Kind of like my face. The swelling was gone now, but the bruising was taking its time to heal. Where Darryl had punched me in the eye was obvious.

Lucas still talked about hunting him down and killing him.

"This is a huge step," Lucas said. "You're my claimed mate now. And I'm yours. It's a much stronger bond than a human marriage or a commitment ceremony. Not even the pack can pull us apart. Only one wolf acknowledged our union, though. My carrier, Adam."

"And everyone else?"

"They're going to take some time to win over."

"I want to be by your side as pack leader."

Lucas rolled to face me and played with the hair over my ear. "I knew you would."

"And not stupid things like filing."

Lucas laughed. "Filing falls to all of us, unfortunately. But I know what you mean. I want your opinion when decisions need to be made. We'll run through everything together."

Good.

That was out of the way.

I nodded. I wasn't sure I could start right away. My mind was still a bit foggy. Maybe I *would* have to begin by filing for a while. I could also help around the cabin. Lucas had wolves come in once a week to clean up after us. It reminded me of Carter and how he had helped me.

I didn't want that in my life anymore.

Hopefully, I was perfectly capable of running a house.

Time would tell.

I turned to face Lucas, shuffled closer to him, and kissed him.

"Love you, my Alpha," I said.

Lucas smiled. "You make my heart sing, Alpha."

Then we were off to the races again. My mate had the kind of stamina I appreciated. Then *much* later, lying in the afterglow of trying to exhaust one another, Lucas clung to my hand.

"Have you given any more thought to meeting Charles and Sandy?"

"They've been playing on my mind."

"I hope you don't mind, but I spoke with Charles. I think he might be your dad's uncle. Is your dad's name Eric Carter?"

A shiver ran through me. I hated hearing that name. "Yeah, that's him."

"Okay, so now we know where Charles fits in."

"And he left to escape the cult?"

"That's what he's confirmed with me. He's glad you're away from them."

"Did you meet with him in person?"

"Only for a few minutes. He seems nice. A bit of dementia, but he also remembers stuff."

I exhaled a long sigh. "Can you give me some more time?"

"All the time you need. You don't even have to meet them. It's up to you."

"Thank you."

"Hey." Lucas kissed me. "Should we take a break and get some breakfast?

"Are you going to try cooked eggs this morning? And a few chunks of yam. I promise they won't kill you. You're perfectly capable of digesting them. Dogs eat them all the time."

Lucas smiled at me. "As long as you're making it, I'll eat whatever you say."

I touched his nose. "Good Alpha."

My mate broke out laughing and rolled me back and forth in a hug as I joined him in laughter. We were both gasping for breath, tears of mirth in our eyes, as we tumbled out of bed.

Breakfast was perfect. Lucas liked everything I fed him.

Claiming one another had brought about a massive shift in our relationship. There would be no end to it other than death. We belonged to one another now.

Carter picked up after a couple of rings. He would have rushed to answer. I didn't phone him very often since Lucas and I started our new journey together.

My best friend probably thought something was wrong.

"What happened?" he started off the call.

I chuckled. So predictable. "Everything is fine." I smiled. "Better than fine."

Carter sighed. He'd been holding his breath. "Are things good with you and Lucas?"

"That's what I was calling about. Lucas and I claimed each other last night."

"Explain exactly what that means?"

"We bit and drank from one another."

"Um ... gross."

"No, it means something in wolf culture. It means we're mated for life."

"Life? Holy shit. Are you serious?"

"We're in love. He's my partner and mate. It was the next step. He even bred with me like a wolf. Details I won't go into. And there was a glimmer of a telepathic link between us."

"I've heard of that with wolves, but you're not a wolf."

"Maybe somewhere along the line, there's wolf in me."

"I doubt it. That would mean inter-species offspring is possible."

A warm rush flowed from my groin up to my chest.

Alpha with Alpha.

If only.

"Maybe it's because we're so close our minds are open to one another."

Carter laughed. "Jesse, I am so happy for you. You have no idea. A mate for life ... all three of us. How did we go from being strung-out street rats to this?"

"Because you had a dream, Carter. I thought it was ludicrous when you suggested we move out of Metro City and find a cabin in the woods. But you made it happen. Even when I was in prison, you kept it going, stashing away the money we would need. You brought the dream to life."

"It wouldn't have happened if you weren't on board. Rory, too. You both trusted me."

"I'm so glad we did. Lucas is my everything."

"You deserve him. After all you did for Rory and me, you deserve every happiness."

My heart pumped faster.

I believed him. I actually believed Carter's words. I was desirable as a mate. Something I never thought would happen to me. I'd lived a psychotic life ... now I'd come home to Lucas.

Lucas, Carter, and Rory were my family.

And there was potentially more of my family close by in Riverton.

A month later, we were sitting outside the Vista Villa care facility in Riverton. It was a predictably cold winter day. I had to decide whether to go inside the building.

Charles Carter knew I was coming. Lucas had called ahead. Whether Charles remembered or not was anyone's guess. Our arrival was timed with when activities ended for the day.

Apparently, Charles really enjoyed bingo, singing, and doing craft projects. We hadn't wanted to interrupt any of those. In two hours, it would be dinner.

I needed to decide.

I grasped the door handle and swung open the truck door. "Okay, let's go do this."

Lucas was right behind me as I went through the front door. My bear sense of smell picked up far too much. A mix of cleaning products, urine, and excrement assaulted me.

I can't believe I'm doing this.

Lucas knew where he was going, and he checked a sitting room first. The bear shifter we were looking for wasn't there, because we continued down the hall to a door at the end.

My mate knocked on that door and then immediately opened it.

Inside, positioned facing a window, sat an elderly male in a wheelchair. Lucas went over to him and put his hand on the male's shoulder. Charles turned his head to look at Lucas.

And gave him a bright smile.

Thank God, he didn't look anything like my dad, except for his pert nose.

Charles patted Lucas's hand, then turned his attention to me. I walked around the end of his bed and stood where he could see me without craning his neck.

"Oh, goodness, you look like your carrier," he said.

I huffed. "Even with the mutton chops." I'd been to a barber when my swelling subsided and had a complete cut and shave. It had felt amazing to be back to looking like myself.

Or my mom, as seemed to be the case.

Made my skin crawl.

"Please don't compare me to her," I said to him. "We're nothing alike."

Charles nodded. "I'm glad to hear that. Your carrier is a vicious shifter."

My nose twitched. "How so?" Not sure why I was asking. Maybe to add fuel to the anger I had toward the parents who had raised me and tried to make me hate myself.

"That dungeon they ran in their basement. She loved punishing errant bear shifters."

Fuck.

"I know the basement well."

Charles closed his eyes and shook his head. "Their own cub. How could they?"

"Because my body wanted to shift. They punished me for it. Made me flog myself every day before school. I had to wear two undershirts to absorb any bleeding I might have."

Lucas filled the room with a rumbling growl.

Charles looked at him. "He's very protective of you, Jesse."

I sucked in my breath. It was the first time he'd said my name. I wasn't sure I liked it on his tongue. He might not look like my dad, but there were glimmers of familiarity in his voice.

Memories tumbled in.

My dad—yelling at me to submit to the life of a human being.

To deny the shift. To punish myself into its non-existence.

"He's my mate," I said after dragging myself back.

Charles's eyebrows lifted. "Two Alphas? A bear and a wolf?"

"We're in love," Lucas replied. "We've claimed one another. We're mates for life."

Charles's gaze went from Lucas to my ring finger. "Married, too?"

"The humans at the chapel didn't know we were shifters," I answered.

Charles chuckled. "Good on you. The stupidest law I've ever heard of—two species of shifter can't marry. Why does it matter to them? It doesn't affect their lives in the slightest."

Then he reached for me. I knew what he wanted, but my feet felt like they were buried in cement. It took a lot of chipping to free them. I walked over and gave him my left hand.

He brushed his fingers over the ring. "I had a love once with a cougar when I was young, before the general population knew we existed. She wanted kits, so it didn't work out."

"I'm sorry to hear that." I thought of Carter and Shaun, a bear and a cougar, and how much they loved each other. Life wasn't going to be easy for them as mates.

Either was ours.

Charles looked from me to Lucas and back again. "I'm so glad you found one another." He released my hand, leaned back, and closed his eyes. His mouth hung open as he fell asleep.

I looked at Lucas, he nodded, and we quietly left the room.

In the hallway, he put his arm around my shoulders. "That turned out all right, didn't it?"

"Yeah, he seems nice enough. I appreciated his approving of us being together."

Lucas kissed the side of my head as we walked. "He's a pioneer for his generation."

"And Sandy, his daughter. Have you talked to her?"

"On the phone. The cabin is on our territory. Charles doesn't own the land, but they're responsible for keeping dead wood cleaned up from the forest floor over three square acres."

"Do you know if she's as liberal as her dad?"

"Her sire says she is."

My cheek twitched. *Dad* was a human word that had been drilled into me. I needed to work on becoming a complete shifter. Lucas would appreciate it if I made the change. I was the partner of a shifter pack leader now. I needed to embrace everything about it.

Sire—not dad.

When we arrived home, Clara was sitting on a stool in the kitchen, eating a sandwich. I still couldn't get used to her being in our home for hours on end each day, lounging on our furniture and eating our food. Lucas told me that's the way things were with Betas helping pack leaders.

She obviously wanted to talk to him.

Clara looked annoyed and impatient.

I was about to go upstairs when someone came through the front door without knocking—another thing I had to get used to. Thankfully, we had hours when wolves could enter our home.

"Can you handle that?" Lucas asked me, pointing at the wolf named Peter.

"Sure thing." I motioned to Peter. "Come into the office."

Peter grunted in annoyance but followed me. I was not, by any stretch, accepted into the pack. It didn't stop me from performing my duties. I took the piece of paper he handed me.

It was a loan application.

Peter wanted to buy a new pickup truck for his business. I signed on to the computer and called up his file. He'd had four loans in the past and kept up with payments on all of them until he paid them off.

I looked at how much he wanted to borrow. It was reasonable for a truck.

I turned to face him. "And you're using this for hauling around building supplies?"

"My old work truck broke down. Wasn't able to fix it."

Okay, so he needed it to continue earning money. He didn't have anything as collateral, like a home, because that wasn't a thing. The pack owned all the houses in the compound.

If you needed one for a growing family, they all pitched in and built one.

Rory's Denver got the contracts to supply the pack with disassembled log homes. I'd seen one go up in my time living with Lucas. The speed at which it was built was stunning.

I retrieved our checkbook from the drawer. I'd been given signing authority last week when Lucas and I attended a bank appointment we'd planned together. I felt comfortable signing checks without Lucas having to look over my shoulder. He trusted me. I even trusted myself.

I reviewed the application to ensure it was filled out correctly, signed the bottom, and wrote a check for the requested amount. When Peter left, I set up the loan on the computer and recorded the check in our accounting software. That had been a slight stumbling block, understanding how to use it. Thankfully, my mate was patient and worked with me until I felt confident with it.

Then I filed the paperwork ... while grumbling at the necessary task.

I was back on my way upstairs when the conversation between Lucas and Clara exploded into a yelling match. I'd never heard Lucas so angry while defending me.

The yelling turned into snarling and snapping. I rushed into the kitchen to break it up before they both did something stupid.

I placed my hands on Lucas's chest and shoved him as hard as I could.

"Chill, Alpha. She's your Beta. Calm down."

"She's not standing by me," he growled.

I looked over my shoulder at Clara, then back at Lucas. "What do you mean?"

"I have challengers for leadership, and she has encouraged them because she doesn't agree with the life I have chosen to lead with the shifter I love."

I dragged my hands down his chest as I studied his eyes. This was my fault. I'd come into Lucas's life and messed things up for him. Now, his leadership was in jeopardy.

"Don't look at me like that," he said to me. "I've chosen you. End of story."

"What about your sire? Has he weighed in?" Lucas Sr. had been the pack leader many years ago. The pack might listen to him. I knew they respected him and his opinions.

"He's been trying to smooth things over, telling the pack you're worthy of the position."

I was glad to hear that. The last I heard, Lucas Sr. wasn't convinced about us as a team. Maybe Adam had finally broken through to him. He'd been in our corner from the beginning.

"What happens next?" I asked.

Lucas looked over my shoulder at Clara. "Set a date and time."

My heart took off running, pounding in my ears, as my limbs went numb. I gripped Lucas's shirt and hauled on it. "For what, Lucas? A date and time for what?"

"I have to fight my challengers."

I shook my head. "No, you can't. Not for me."

I sensed movement behind me, then the front door slammed. We were alone ... for now.

"Jesse ...." Lucas stroked my cheek. "I would give it all up for you. The entire leadership of the pack. Surely, you know that. Nothing is more important to me than you."

I believed him.

I relaxed my grip on his shirt. "You could get hurt ... killed even."

Lucas smiled at me. "That last bit won't happen, I can guarantee you that. There's a reason our lineage has been in leadership for so long."

I set my forehead on his chin. That's how much bigger he was than me. I'd seen very few wolf shifters as big as my mate. He was right. The immense ones I'd seen were all related to him.

I gripped his massive biceps and felt better.

The love of my life would survive this.

On the day of the challenges, I was exhausted. I hadn't slept in days. Lucas, on the other hand, had snored his way through the lead up to the fight for his life and leadership.

He wasn't worried.

I shouldn't be either.

The fighting would take place directly in front of our cabin. Lucas told me I was to stay on the porch, out of the danger zone. We stood on the inside of our front door, hand in hand.

Lucas opened it, and we emerged as a united front. I was his chosen mate.

For life.

Regardless of what happened today.

I stayed behind on the porch as Lucas descended the steps in the nude, into a circle of wolves in their human form. Three were naked males. Those were his challengers.

Lucas would have to fight them one after another.

One stepped forward into the circle, and Lucas steadied himself. He was immediately put on the defensive when the challenger launched himself at Lucas. My mate had told me it had to be this way. He couldn't be the first to attack. His role was to respond to the challenge.

They tumbled to the ground, wrestling in the damp dirt and gravel. It had rained this morning and would likely start up again, making bare skin slippery. I jerked with each blow they threw at each other. There were no rules of play. No limit to how much damage they could do.

I clenched my fists as the fight continued. I desperately wanted to jump in and defend my mate's birthright. I had no place doing so. This was Lucas's fight.

Back on their feet, they grappled, trying to gain dominance. It sounded like a drumbeat each time they collided. My mate maintained the upper hand as the challenger dug at his eyes.

The fight was raw and dirty—and exhilarating.

I heard the crack before I registered what happened. Lucas's opponent's arm hung at an unnatural angle. Lucas had snapped the large bone in two. It was sticking through the skin.

Lucas growled and surged forward, and the challenger backed away and left the circle. My mate was sweaty and his chest heaving with the effort it had taken to win this round.

Challenger number two stepped into the circle.

He was smaller than Lucas and didn't last long. This time, it was a femur that was broken. The amount of force it had taken to destroy that bone was thrilling.

Both my stomach and my cock tingled.

He was my mate.

He was mine, and he was incredible and sexy beyond words.

The next challenger entered the circle in wolf form. I'd spotted him as Peter earlier. He afforded Lucas enough time to shift before running at him. He was as big as Lucas. I clenched the railing as they barked, snarled, and snapped, and tried to get a hold on one another with their teeth.

Peter secured the front of Lucas's neck in his jaws, and Lucas yipped, then fought until he pulled away. He went after Peter harder, knocking him over. I hadn't realized Lucas had been holding back. Peter didn't stand a chance. He soon whimpered, cried, and crept away.

Lucas's fur receded, then he shifted back, his body contorting into its human form. He looked up at me and motioned for me to join him. I jogged down the steps to be by his side.

He reached for my hand, and I felt intense relief as he clasped it. Other than two puncture wounds in his neck and some scratches, my mate was intact. He raised his other hand.

The murmuring in the crowd subsided.

"Jesse is my chosen mate. We have claimed each other, and we are mated for life. I have met and fought with the challengers who sought to overthrow my leadership. Challenges that stem from my love for this Alpha bear shifter. The opposition to him and me ends here and now."

A few of the crowd grunted and left, but most remained. One by one, they entered the circle, bowed their head to Lucas, and left, until we were the only ones standing there.

Aside from Clara.

She stared at Lucas, then bowed her head and kept it down. "Alpha."

Lucas walked to her, touched her chin, and lifted her head to look at him. "You don't need to stay with me if you're uncomfortable doing so. You have served our family well for years."

Clara nodded. "I think I'm going to retire." Then she looked at me and back to Lucas. "I've been watching your mate in his duties. He has the fortitude and skill to be of benefit to you."

I touched my chest.

Lucas exhaled. "Thank you for saying that."

"It saddens me that there are no pups in your future."

I frowned. It saddened me, too. No cubs or pups of any kind would come into our lives, but we would have *us*. And that was more than enough.

"Maddox will have plenty of pups to take over leadership," Lucas said.

Clara nodded.

"Thank you for all you've done, Beta," Lucas added.

Clara gave him a weak smile, then walked into Lucas's open arms and joined him in a moving, final hug. I'm glad that it happened. It was closure for them both.

Lucas and I would be on our own until we could find another Beta.

Until then, we would manage.

I felt pride as we walked back into our home.

CHAPTER 13

LUCAS

The warm, amber glow from the cabin's interior lights through the front windows made me feel like I was truly coming home. There was even the scent of earthy woodsmoke in the air.

A wash of welcome heat hit me immediately as I walked into the foyer. Jesse had stoked up the fireplace to keep out the winter cold. I brushed the snow off my coat, hung it on a hook near the front door, stomped the snow off my boots, and removed them.

"Hey," Jesse called from the kitchen. "Dinner is almost ready. Take a seat by the fire. I've spread out a soft, cozy blanket. Thought we could eat picnic style."

I'd called Jesse earlier to let him know I'd be late. I'd been waiting for hours for a delivery of light fixtures for the new house we were wiring. It was almost eight in the evening.

I'd missed him.

"Did you get much pack business today?" I asked.

Our home was open to our pack wolves from nine until seven at night. Jesse would have had to deal with everyone on his own all day today. And then again, when I should've been here.

"There was a dispute about a borrowed snow blower of all things."

I walked into the kitchen. Jesse was busy cutting up a beef steak into cubes at the counter. I crowded up against his body and kissed the back of his head. "Did you set them straight?"

"Had to march out to Eric's in a blizzard to make him give the damned thing back."

"Did he give you any grief?"

"Snarled at me and called me *bear* as if it was some kind of insult." Jesse arranged the beef cubes on a wooden platter with cups of raw eggs and some frozen blueberries. "I reminded him that when I'm shifted, I'm bigger than him and could knock him on his ass."

I smiled and chuckled.

"Sounds like an eventful day."

Jesse grunted. "If they think they can push me around, they have another thing coming."

I hugged him around his waist. "I love you."

"I love you, too ... and your deep love for me." Jesse fussed with the food on the wooden platter, then turned to face me. "I'm nervous about meeting Sandy tomorrow."

"Are you sure you don't want a ride?"

Jesse smiled at me. "I'm perfectly capable of managing a drive to Riverton." His eyes were a shocking blue this evening. The color always deepened when he was feeling confident.

"Do you want to borrow my truck?"

"No, my old beast will get me there just fine."

Since I was at work during the day, we bought Jesse a gently used SUV so he could get to his daily dose at the pharmacy. The snow was deep and treacherous this far into the mountains. Four-wheel drive was imperative, and I'd taught him how to put on chains if he needed to.

"And you're *sure* you don't want me to come with you."

Jesse placed his hand on my chest. "Stop. I'll be all right. You have fun with Maddox."

My brother was in Creekside for a couple of days, visiting family and showing off their firstborn pup. She was only three months old and already exhibiting aggressive Alpha qualities.

I saw pack leadership in her future.

Maddox and I planned to head into the woods for a hunt tomorrow afternoon while Jesse was away, meeting Sandy and more of his family. I cupped his handsome, kissable face.

"They're going to love you."

Jesse smirked. "You're biased, husband."

"Maybe." I stepped away. "Now, how is this picnic going to work?"

"It'll be fun." Jesse took the platter, and I followed him into the living room, where he set the food down on a blanket spread out in front of the fire.

I sat on it beside him, gazing into the flames, then into his eyes.

"Is this picnic going to end with *dessert*?"

Jesse pretended to look shocked. Hand at his throat—eyes wide. The whole theatrical thing. "Are you propositioning me to have sex with you in front of the fire?"

I ran my fingers down his arm. "Before or after ... it's up to you."

Jesse bit his bottom lip, lost in my gaze, then pushed the platter aside.

"You know ... I'm not so hungry for food after all."

"Mm." I angled my body, cradled his jawline, and kissed him. He leaned against me and urged me backward onto the blanket, his lips never leaving mine.

Slowly and deliberately, we worked our way out of our clothes until we were nude, our skin being warmed by the roaring fire. Jesse growled as I positioned myself between his thighs and sucked his cock into my mouth. The taste of his flesh was what I'd been craving all day.

I'd come home to him—my partner in all things.

My mate for life.

Jesse gripped handfuls of the blanket as my lips and tongue rode him until he was grunting and digging his fingers into my hair as he came, filling my throat with his seed.

A quick tumble in reverse, and we were both left panting, staring up at the ceiling. Our cocks fulfilled for the time being. Jesse laughed. "We really should eat."

"Sounds perfect."

Jesse let out a soft *fuck* as I flipped him over onto his stomach, spread his legs, and dove face first into his ass. I didn't fuck him until my tongue had him whining and crying out for me.

We eventually ate, feeding one another and lounging in front of the flames. I wanted moments like this to go on forever. Two Alphas sharing the making of everlasting memories.

Loving each other.

When we dragged ourselves to bed, we'd both been thoroughly fucked.

Jessie left plenty of time to get to Sandy's in Riverton. I had watched him head off down the driveway. He'd already been out in the morning, getting his daily dose of methadone, and fared just fine, but the snow was coming down hard, so I was slightly apprehensive. I had suggested Jesse postpone the get-together, but he wouldn't hear of it.

His Alpha male had come out forceful.

I knew not to argue with him in that state.

He'd been getting stronger with each passing day. Staying sober and talking with his therapist by video call twice a week was both hard on him but ultimately healing in the end.

I was so proud of my mate.

The sound of the front door opening preceded a rush of cold air into the cabin. Either it was a pack wolf looking for something, or my brother Maddox had arrived.

His scent nearly overpowered me.

It was the latter.

My brother barged in and took a seat across from me in the office.

"Ready to do this hunt?" he asked.

He looked excited. Living in Metro City must be hard for a wolf used to shifting at least once a week—usually more. I wondered if he shifted in their apartment for release.

Maddox must really love Laura to give up everything Creekside had to offer. Her existence had pulled at him, like a fated mate, from the time he met her during his monthly gathering with his university buddies in Metro City. Lucas Sr. had insisted that every one of his offspring attend university. I had excelled at getting a business degree. Maddox had a degree in law.

"Are you sure we want to trek through this snow?" I asked.

"We've done it before." Maddox crossed his arms. "Please don't bail on me."

"I'm worried about Jesse. What if he calls?"

"Give your phone to Adam. He can field any calls for you."

I exhaled long and hard. That would work. Adam could contact me through our wolf pack's link if Jesse called and needed something from me. Even with a link established between Jesse and me, he was unable to connect with the pack, and he rarely let me in. He wanted to protect me from the turmoil that still tore up his mind. It hurt, but I agreed to respect his privacy.

If things were really bad and he needed my support, I hoped he would reach out to me without using a phone, but he'd been quite adamant. He wasn't ready for our mind link yet.

"All right," I replied.

Maddox clapped his hands together once. "Excellent!"

I was warm in my winter gear as we walked to our sire's cabin, but I'd be shedding it soon to shift. I wasn't looking forward to the blast of cold air, the wind whipping around my bare body.

Adam opened the door when Maddox knocked.

I held out my phone to him. "Can you take any calls on my phone and transmit the information to me if it's Jesse in trouble ... or *not* in trouble but needing to talk to me?"

"Sure thing." Adam accepted the phone. "What's the code?"

"161616."

Adam smirked. "Hardly cryptic."

I smiled at him. My carrier, Adam, was the best. He'd given us an incredible upbringing. A perfect mix of discipline and fun. He and my sire had nurtured us into strong wolves.

A blast of cold, snowy wind whipped past us.

It would be lovely if Adam invited us in for a warm drink instead, but it was time to strip off. We did so on their front porch, and Adam took our clothes inside to keep them warm by the fire for when we shifted back. I was thankful for the dense fur as it covered my body.

Both my brother and I were immense wolves. Members of our pack, out shovelling, stepped back to let us pass. Maddox took off, loping through the deep snow. Once we reached the forest, there would be less snow on the ground, the undergrowth protected by the trees' canopy.

It was easy going as we headed north toward the outskirts of our territory. The elk and deer knew better than to live anywhere near our compound of houses. We had to travel for them.

Made me slightly nervous, being so far from our cabin and my truck.

The more I travelled, though, the more the thoughts of Jessie left my mind, my wolf mind taking over. I was focused on reaching our destination and catching a scent.

Fully in wolf mode, we arrived and immediately caught the musk of a male elk. We picked our way through the trees until we found him. He was young but substantial.

Maddox circled around and took up a position across from me, in front of the elk, the breeze not exposing either one of us. My approach would startle him straight toward my brother, who would latch onto his throat while I took up the rear and incapacitated the tendons on his rear legs.

We executed the takedown without fault, and Maddox finished him off.

The only way to get him back to the compound was to shift to human form and carry him out. We would be practically hypothermic by the time we reached our sire's home and our fireplace warmed clothes. Maddox sent a message to everyone asking for a hand.

Clothed pack members with a sled reached us halfway back and took over carting the elk home, so Maddox and I were able to shift into the comfort of our thick fur.

We arrived back ahead of the group and went into the butcher's shed. It was barely warmer than outside. We shifted and arranged the knives, then went to be reunited with our clothes.

We were partway through dressing the elk when my phone rang.

It was Sandy.

"Is everything all right?" I answered.

"No. I'm not sure what's happening. I offered to put some Irish Cream liquor in Jesse's coffee, and he got really quiet, then started trembling. He's holding his stomach and rocking. He keeps telling us he's all right ... but he's not. I wasn't sure what to do. He suggested calling you."

Sandy finally took a breath.

"I'll be there in an hour." I knew it might take longer than that, but I was going to drive as fast as I could while remaining safe. I would be no use to Jesse if I ended up in the ditch.

"What do I do until then?"

"Keep assuring him I'm on my way. That might settle him."

"Okay. See you soon."

I needed to get to my Alpha. He hadn't been around alcohol since he started his recovery. He must be fighting hard to block the longing. Maybe I should have told Sandy he's an alcoholic.

Except, it wasn't my life story to tell.

If Jesse wanted her to know, he'd share that with her.

The snow kept coming down as I drove. The plows had been through, but the highway was being covered faster than they could keep up. It was almost two hours before I arrived.

I shielded my face from the blowing snow as I knocked on Sandy's door. She ushered me straight in. Jesse was wrapped in a blanket, bent forward, and nursing a fruity tea.

He was safe.

But he was in no state to drive.

Jessie was pale and clammy, and his eyes registered a massive amount of relief at seeing me. Standing and seated in Sandy's living room with her were her husband and their two kids.

All eyes were on Jesse.

He must be feeling incredibly uncomfortable.

I took the tea from his hands and set it on the coffee table. "Let's get you home."

Jesse frowned but threw off the blanket and stood. The outward vulnerability he had been expressing when I first walked in turned to anger. I could detect the scent of it on him.

He pushed me aside, rushed into the front entry, and yanked on his coat and boots. I turned to Sandy. "Thank you so much for calling me. Jesse was really nervous to meet you."

"I hope he feels better, so he can come back. I don't have any other cousins."

"I'm sure he will."

Jesse flung open the front door.

"That's my cue," I said to Sandy and took off after Jesse. I found him next to his SUV and cringed when he punched a dent into it. He was furious at himself.

Definitely not driving.

We could pick up his vehicle later in the week, once the snow abated. He began challenging me with his eyes. He'd have to fight me if he wanted to drive himself home.

Thankfully, he had enough sense to climb into my truck. Seatbelt on, he crossed his arms and put his head against the window, scowling and muttering.

As I pulled onto the highway, Jesse's muttering turned into words.

"I'm a fucking idiot junkie."

"A bit harsh."

He glared at me. "I don't get why you want to be with me."

"Because I love you."

Jesse stared through his passenger window. "That makes no sense to me. I couldn't even be around alcohol without having a meltdown. I'm never going to be better."

"You already are. It's been months since you used. You're doing amazing in your recovery."

Jesse harrumphed. "They must think I'm deranged."

"They don't. Sandy wants to see you again."

I glanced over at Jesse. His eyes were closed, and he was shaking his head. "It feels so easy to slip. I wanted that alcohol in my coffee so bad."

"But you didn't have any, did you? Surely, you see that as progress."

Jesse grunted and shrugged his shoulders. I wasn't going to be able to convince him that he was worthy of sobriety and love today. Today, he wanted to wallow in embarrassment and anger.

When we arrived home, Jessie stripped off on the front porch, shifted, and headed for the woods. I didn't go after him. He would come back when he was ready to.

Chapter 14

JESSE

I blundered through the forest as my mind buzzed, screaming at me that I was a worthless piece of shit and was of no use to anyone, especially Lucas.

His love for me made no sense.

I was a junkie, and junkies eventually fucked up.

I snorted as I ran.

My heart would never recover if I were separated from Lucas.

I needed to trust my Alpha to do what was best for *him*.

It took far too many seconds for me to realize the scents around me had changed. Wolves marked their territory with urine and by rubbing their scent glands on trees.

I was no longer smelling Lucas's pack.

I'd crossed the boundary into West Creekside territory. I tried to convince myself I didn't care, but I did. Even though East Creekside hadn't accepted me, they were still my pack.

I was in a leadership role alongside my mate.

Breaking the rules was out of the question, so I crossed back, but it was too late. A chorus of howling broke the silence of the trees. They'd caught my scent. If they came to investigate, the West Creekside pack would detect that I had strayed onto their side of the boundary.

I was backing up when another sound caught my attention—the growling of a small animal. I turned toward the bushes and used my snout to push branches aside; the creature barked at me.

Her scent was unmistakable. This was a young pup from East Creekside.

How the hell she had wandered this far away was a mystery. Surely, her sire was out looking for her. The rival pack's howling sounded closer. Maybe it was the pup they were after.

She charged out of the bushes and glared up at me. She was a feisty little Alpha. A valuable asset if West Creekside wanted to redraw boundaries with East Creekside.

I snuffled her head.

She almost smelled like Lucas.

I took a step back. This was Maddox's new pup, Maisie.

My pack must be frantic. Surely, they'd be here soon.

Not soon enough. Wolves surrounded us, stepping ever closer with their heads lowered, growling. I picked Maisie up by the scruff and dumped her in a hollow under a nearby tree.

I growled and snapped at her to implore her to stay put.

She grumbled but sat on her haunches, leaving me to face the wolf pack. My fierce protective Alpha male fury came out full force as I turned and thundered toward them.

They were not going to capture or kill this pup.

Not today.

Not ever.

The first two wolves launched themselves at me. My instincts took over, and I swatted them aside, yelping but then regrouping. They were testing me. I roared and stood on my hind legs.

I was enormous compared to them, but they weren't going to back down.

Four wolves crept toward me, and I dropped back on my forefeet, shaking the ground. I spun around as they encircled me, then attacked. Two were on my back, biting me while I battled another. Out of the corner of my eye, I caught sight of the fourth heading for the tree hollow.

I shuffled back, taking the wolves clinging to me with me, then whipped around, dislodging them. With an incredible swing of my arm, my claws caught the wolf who was attempting to steal Maisie across the throat, opening it. He whined and stumbled, then fell, bleeding out.

Maisie poked her head out as more wolves attacked me. I used my paw to push her further into the hollow and engaged with the assault. As soon as I threw one wolf off, another would take its place, snapping and snarling, and sinking their fangs into my flesh.

I was vicious and frantic in my response, standing on any wolves that landed near me, while spinning and swatting at others. I knew I was bleeding, but I would never back down.

They'd have to kill me to get to Maisie.

I lowered my inner defenses and, in my mind, called out to Lucas that I was with Maisie. That I was tiring but holding. That I loved him and was prepared to die for this member of our pack.

Lucas's voice whispered through me.

"We're coming. Stay strong."

Then a brief pause.

"I love you, too, my Alpha."

I slashed and fought, on all fours and standing, towering over them. While I was engaged, other solitary wolves kept trying to slip behind me to reach the hollow and Maisie. I kept myself backed up to it and flicked snow into it to stop her every time I sensed Maisie surging forward.

I groaned with relief when the East Creekside pack flew into the fray. There were three times as many of our wolves as there were of theirs, and we soon had the rivals running.

Knowing Maisie was safe, I collapsed, breathing heavy. The pain began creeping in from the bite and claw marks all over my body. Lucas was beside me, shifted to human form.

"Alpha, we need to help you," he said. "We can't do that while you're shifted."

I shook my head. It was cold, and I was severely injured. I stood more of a chance of making it home without faltering and succumbing to my wounds if I stayed in bear form.

Maddox and Laura were whining near my rear. While fighting to protect Maisie, I'd covered the hollow under the tree with my hind end. I struggled to my feet and moved away.

Maddox retrieved their bundle of love, picking her up by her scruff. I sensed that Maddox and his mate were scolding their pup while telling her they loved her. They looked up at me, then bowed their heads to me. I wasn't sure what the action meant, but I knew it held meaning.

Lucas shifted beside me into wolf form and rubbed his furry head on my snout. It was then, as I raised my head from his affection, that I was aware of the wolves in our pack all standing around us, staring at me. It started with one wolf. He jogged off, then came back with a stick.

And set it in front of me.

One after another, what I soon realized was an honor, was repeated until every wolf in our pack had laid a stick in front of me. Lucas rubbed against me again and spoke in my mind.

"The pack has embraced your leadership as my mate. The laying of the sticks means they will lay down their life to protect you. Your place is with us ... forever."

If I'd been in human form, I would be struggling to hold in tears.

The best I could do was bow my head to them in acknowledgement of their pledge to me. I wished I could take the sticks with me, but I understood their profound meaning belonged in the forest that was our home. This territory was ours, and I was now truly part of its stewardship.

The howling began shortly after the last wolf backed away from me. It was deafening and glorious as it filled the forest. Beside me, Lucas's howl was loudest ... and so filled with love.

I wished I could join them.

The best I could do was growl. One by one, silence fell upon us.

I needed to get home.

Wolves surrounded me as I lumbered toward our cabin, limping and breathing heavy through the pain. I was exhausted by the time we reached home. Lucas supported me after I shifted to human form and stumbled in through our front door. My legs gave out in the front entry.

The tiles were cold beneath my bare skin as I slipped from his arms.

I didn't object or fuss when Lucas lifted me, settled me on the rug in front of the fire, and stoked the flames until they were throwing off some heat. I lay still as the dead.

My mind had gone hazy from the pain and exertion. I closed my eyes as Lucas began cleansing my wounds with a cotton ball and some rubbing alcohol. The scent burned my nostrils, but didn't trigger me. He turned me back and forth until he had attended to them all.

"They're mostly puncture wounds. You've got tough skin when you're a bear." Lucas ran his fingers through my hair. "What you did for Maisie ... I'll never take your sacrifice for granted."

"I would've died protecting her."

Lucas leaned forward and kissed my forehead. "My forever mate, I know you would."

A warm glow shone in through the windows, and I could hear increasingly louder chatter and laughter. The pack had assembled outside around a bonfire—a celebration. I had forgotten that Lucas and Maddox had gone hunting today. They must have brought something back.

Before the bulk of the kill was packaged and put in our freezer, the pack would share strips of its flesh as a united, thriving pack. I wasn't sure I could drag myself outside to partake.

"Let's start with some bandages," Lucas said and left for the kitchen. He came back with our first aid box and expertly patched me up, so any bleeding wounds were covered.

I was so weak that I could barely drag myself to sit.

Lucas gave me the most incredible, caring, and loving kiss, then headed upstairs. He brought down a fleecy sweatshirt and pants and helped me into them.

I groaned as Lucas helped me to my feet and wrapped a blanket around my shoulders. I needed to make an appearance. I knew that, but it didn't stop my body from objecting as Lucas led me onto the front porch and down the steps to the bonfire.

He only left me struggling to stand on my own for a few seconds as he pulled a chair off the porch and set it behind me to sit in. I'd be permitted that concession by the pack.

With everyone assembled, two pack members, carrying wooden platters piled high with meat, made the rounds. It smelled like elk. And tasted sublime as I chewed on the chunk I'd been given.

From across the circle, Maddox and his mate, Laura, made their way to us with little Maisie in Laura's arms. She was squirming, barking, and being a general nuisance.

I wasn't surprised she had managed to give her sire and carrier the slip. She was a handful of courageous, adventurous pup. Lucas felt she would become our next pack leader.

"We want to thank you again," Maddox said. "You risked your life for our pup."

Laura nodded. "We'll be forever grateful and forever in your debt."

Before I could answer, they turned back to the gathered group and crossed to the other side. I tugged the blanket tighter around me to shield me from the cold at my back. Lucas, always in tune with me now, moved behind me to protect me. He placed his hands on my shoulders.

His love for me was profound.

As I looked around the bonfire at our pack, there were many pups in both stages of shift. Older pups in human form danced around the fire, giggling while younger pups nipped at their heels.

I touched my chest above my heart. I'd been awoken by a dream last week.

One where we had a young cub barreling around our home.

And a young pup by their side.

Except, it had felt like more than a dream.

I needed to talk to Carter.

The milkshake I'd ordered tasted like sawdust in my mouth through no fault of any menu items at Growlers. I was nervous, and my body felt like it was malfunctioning.

I had considered telling Lucas I had arranged this meeting with Carter, but decided I wanted to be able to bring information back to him rather than build his hopes and then not be able to deliver. I wasn't ready yet, but when I was, this would be a massive step.

Carter limped up to the booth I was in. "Your message was cryptic." He slid in across from me and picked up a menu, perused it, then looked at me. "You not eating?"

"My stomach would object." I pushed the shake aside. "Can't even drink this."

Carter snagged it, pulled it to him, and sucked a long draw of milkshake into his mouth. It was an old habit of ours. Finishing what food the other could not. It screamed of survival mode; something we had left behind. But some old ways were hard to abandon.

"So ...." Carter tapped his fingers on the table. "Why am I here?"

"Thought we could catch up."

Carter's brow dipped, and he narrowed his eyes, suspicious. "We talk most days on the phone." He was right. I had started calling him more often. Rory, too. Now that my methadone dose was at a maintenance level and my body had acclimated to it, I'd been more communicative.

Might as well jump right in.

"I have a question to ask you."

Carter leaned back. "Okay. Shoot."

I cleared my throat. "As you know, Lucas and I are in a committed relationship. We have claimed one another, and the pack has accepted me ... but we can't produce offspring."

"That doesn't sound like a question."

Fucking hell, this is hard.

"You're an Omega."

Now, Carter's brow really furrowed. "And ...?"

Spit it out.

"Would you be open to having a cub with me?"

Carter released a short, sharp laugh and crossed his arms. "Wow."

My heart was thundering so hard, I was getting a piercing headache. It seemed as though I'd stepped too far and asked too much of my best friend. I should've approached Rory instead.

Except, I didn't want a cub with Rory.

Carter stared at me, his chest rising and falling like mad. "How would that work?"

I sucked in a quick breath. I couldn't believe he was considering it. I hadn't worked out the details of wanting to have a cub in our lives—Lucas, me ... and Carter and Shaun.

"We would have joint custody."

Carter tipped his head.

"In vitro?"

"Whatever would make you most comfortable."

Carter shrugged. "I'd be open to either way."

My face flushed, and it felt as if my heart might burst out of my ears; it was pounding so hard. Carter was asking about the details and considering my monumental proposal.

"Joint custody for sure, right?" he asked.

"Fifty-fifty. The cub would consider the four of us to be their primary protectors."

His brow crunched briefly. "I would need to talk to Shaun."

"Of course. I haven't even spoken to Lucas yet."

Carter chewed on his bottom lip, then released it. "For the record ... *I'm* all for it."

I leapt up from my seat, grinning, and launched myself at Carter, hugging him. He laughed and hugged me back, then patted my shoulders. "Okay ... okay ... calm down."

Dropping back into my seat, I couldn't stop smiling. Having a cub with someone I loved and bringing that cub into the life of my forever mate, who held my heart, was beyond wondrous.

I reached across the table. Carter hesitated but then took my hands. "When?" he asked.

"I'm not ready yet," I said. "I need to focus on myself before introducing a cub into our lives."

"I was going to bring that up."

"I will reach that milestone in my life, though. I'm getting stronger every day."

Carter smiled at me. "I know you are, and I am so proud of you ... Alpha."

I hummed, hearing that word from him. If we had a cub together, I would be an acting Alpha in Carter's life. I knew he and Shaun alternated in that role. Carter had spoken of it, and I would never want to interfere. This decision required both Carter and Shaun to be fully on board.

"I won't mention anything to Lucas until you tell me it's all right," he said.

"I'll talk to him soon."

Carter smiled. "I'm going to tell Shaun as soon as I get home."

My heart sang, and I left Growlers feeling lighter and more hopeful. My entire life was truly in Creekside now. I was tied to this land and this community—bears, wolves, and cougars.

My heart would reside here until it beat no more.

CHAPTER 15

LUCAS

B y the end of the day, we would be finished with the house we'd been working on for the past week. The number of new home builds in Creekside Valley was increasing. Between those and the other electrical work from Creekside to Riverton, Black Electric was thriving.

It had been a struggle to switch from electric work during the day to pack business in the evenings until Jesse stepped into his role. Now, he was handling most of the pack's affairs.

There were still decisions to be made, and we made those together after discussion. Of course, I still held veto power, but we had yet to reach any impasse requiring it.

Jesse was a strong and intelligent leader.

Carter limped into the dining room where I was working on outlets, and he was smiling. He'd been practically giddy for weeks. I wasn't sure what had gotten into him. He and Jesse had been talking more recently, but Jesse hadn't mentioned anything that would warrant—

"What the hell are you so happy about?"

Carter leaned against a window frame. "Nothing in particular."

"I've never seen you like this. What gives? Are you and Shaun pregnant or something?"

He laughed, as he'd done many times before, but there was an extra glimmer in his eye.

Carter was aggravating me. "Seriously? What?"

He waved his hand at me. "It's nothing. Things are going particularly well between Shaun and me. Jesse is killing it with his recovery, and Rory is beyond blissful. I'm feeling full."

I wasn't sure that Carter was telling me everything, but I played along.

"After what you've all been through, you deserve happiness."

"I believe that now. Didn't use to, and it took me a long time to get here, but I do."

"You're feeling settled and complete."

Carter shrugged. "Almost."

"Cubs?"

"Yeah, it's hard. Shaun and I would love to be surrounded by cubs and kits."

"Maybe someday."

Carter smirked at me. "Maybe."

Seriously? What's he smirking about?

Before I could question Carter further, he left to finish the installation of the kitchen island's pendant lighting. Maybe Jesse would know what was up with Carter.

At home, I tried bringing it up with Jesse, but he was evasive.

They were up to something.

When the weekend arrived, Jesse and I drove to Riverton to try again to meet with his family. Carter and I had collected Jesse's SUV a couple of weeks ago when we had work out that way.

Thankfully, the roads were plowed, and the sun was shining low in the bright blue sky. It was the perfect day for a drive. The trees at the edge of the road were covered in snow and glistening.

It felt like my first ever Christmas. The only one that had ever truly mattered.

This Christmas, I would be spending it with my forever love.

You couldn't get much more festive than that.

I sat beside Jesse as he chatted with Sandy and Charles, sharing some aspects of his childhood and life with them. Mainly the happy stuff. Jesse had found joy where he could. His friends in school. Riding his bike as a kid. Even building an awesome shelter in a protected alleyway and making a deal with the city's best deli owners to allow him to dumpster dive their delicacies.

His family was respectful in their responses and felt open to asking questions.

The conversation flowed.

Jesse reached for my hand, and I held it on my thigh.

"When I visited you," Jesse began, his gaze on Sandy. "I had an issue with the alcohol you offered me. That's why I freaked out and had to leave. I wasn't long into my recovery." He squeezed my hand. "I'm a drug addict and an alcoholic. I've been working really hard to remain sober."

Sandy clasped her hands together and leaned forward. "You could have told us."

"We'd only just met," Jesse replied.

"Jesse ... you're family." Sandy smiled at him. "We're here for you no matter what."

Jesse chuckled. "Don't go saying that. My life hasn't been exactly PG-13."

Charles laughed. "Well, we don't need to hear that bit. You're with us now. That's all that matters. You got away from the *Children of Eleutheria*, and you found shifter love."

Jesse looked over at me and smiled. "I certainly did."

"Well ...." Charles wheeled himself forward. "Dinner bell is going to ring soon."

"Yeah." Jesse stood. "Yeah, we should get going."

"Not before you give me a hug," Sandy said and walked toward him. Jesse wrapped his arms around her, and they clung to one another as if reuniting with their best friend after years apart.

Sandy kissed Jesse's cheek.

I heard her whisper, "Love you." It made my heart swim with happiness.

"Love you, too," Jesse whispered back.

He gave her another tight squeeze, then retreated to embrace Charles. When Jesse took a step back, I could see that Charles was crying—and smiling; the reunion had brought him comfort.

My mate was quiet for the entire ride home, likely replaying everything that had been shared and discussed with his newly found family. They were a piece in making his life feel whole.

I wanted that for Jesse.

A fulfilling life carried along by our love for one another.

When we entered our cabin, there were a few pack members in our kitchen, rearranging our deep freeze to accommodate what smelled like moose meat wrapped in butcher paper.

It was a perk of being the pack leader. Our freezer was never empty. We had as much meat as we could use, provided by those who formed our hunting parties.

After they left, I locked the door, even though it wasn't time to do so. I didn't want anyone else in our home. My Alpha needed decompression time after the day's events.

Except that he had other ideas.

Jesse walked into my arms and kissed me. The kind of kiss that rocketed pure desire up and down my spine, and made my cock take serious notice.

His eyes glistened, and were blue as the deepest northern ice when he took a breath and held my face in both hands, studying mine. My eyes, my lips, my evident, intense love for him.

"Make love to me," he whispered, then slid one hand down to mine and led me upstairs. He took a few steps into our bedroom, stripped off his shirt over his head, and dropped it to the floor.

I kept my distance as I walked past him and sat on the end of the bed. He had that glimmer in his eyes when he wanted to undress and put on a show for me while I watched.

Jesse swung his hips back and forth as he draped his arms up over his head, licking his lips, then parting them, creating a space I longed to have around my dick.

He brushed the flat of his hands down his chest to his abs, then caressed, circled, and pinched his nipples while moaning—his hips still rocking and gyrating. His cock was swollen and stiff, and taking up a broad space almost all the way to the band of his jeans.

My mate had been abundantly gifted.

I loved to feel him gliding inside me.

Wanting to move this forward, I removed my shirt and cupped my hard dick through my pants, and caressed it while keeping eye contact with Jesse. He groaned and tipped his chin up as he flicked his attention from my eyes to the movement of my hand and unlatched his belt.

Ever so slowly, he dragged his jeans and underwear down his legs until he was able to step out of them. A quick shift of his weight back and forth to take off his socks, and he stood nude in front of me, the most perfect and beautiful creature I'd ever laid eyes on.

His chest heaved up and down as he waited for me to remove the rest of my clothes. He jutted his chin up without a word, motioning for me to scoot up the bed.

Once I was comfortable with a pillow behind my head, Jesse approached the foot of the bed, then crawled onto it. I felt as if a wild animal was stalking me as he crept up my body.

I closed my eyes and let myself float on our love as he kissed me. He placed his hands on either side of my head and endeavored to devour my mouth, his lips and tongue possessive as he rubbed his dick against mine by thrusting his hips up and back.

After pulling away, leaving me breathless, Jesse shifted forward, rose on his knees, and sank my cock all the way into his body in one swift motion. He loved an unprepped fuck.

My mate was slick past his hole, giving credence to our belief that Alphas were meant to be penetrated as much as Omegas. Our bodies fit perfectly together.

I grasped his hips, my thumbs on the prominent bones, and rode along with his rise and fall. I focused on his dick bouncing above my stomach, precum leaking from the tip. I let my gaze wander over every curve and contour of his body, groaning, from his firm abs to his muscular chest.

Everywhere, pink and purple marks decorated his skin, reminders of his bravery and his willingness to die for our pack. The scars would fade with time, but not the courageous deed that had put them there. He was the rightful mate of a pack leader in every way possible.

I licked my lips and clung tighter to him, my dick throbbing.

Jesse's nipples were hard and fat and begging for me to suck on them. Above them, Jesse's collarbones were prominent and lickable. Higher, I could see the scars where I had bitten him.

Where I had claimed him as my forever mate.

I brushed my fingers across it, then traced his skin up to his jaw. He was breathing heavy, with his eyes closed, head tipped back, riding me hard, with his hands on my chest.

I growled, clung to his back, and rolled us over until I was above him. That earned me a cheeky smile from him. He wrapped his legs around my waist and put his heels on my ass, guiding me to thrust high and slow, loving him. Each thrust of my hips brought tears to his brilliant eyes.

This was more than sex.

This was an enduring connection that had started in that hotel room in Metro City. The first time I told him I loved him. Somehow, my heart knew what Jesse would come to mean to me.

I grunted with each meaningful undulation of my hips, my ass clenching, my thumbs wiping away the tears before they reached his ears as they rolled down Jesse's skin.

My body, sensing Jesse was my true mate, began to knot, the base of my dick swelling. Jesse murmured, "Yes ... yes," as I stretched him wide with my knotted girth until I was stuck and couldn't shift out of his body. My pelvic floor lifted, and I released my seed high into my love.

As I gazed down at his beauty, Jesse panted and grunted and constricted my cock as he spilled onto his stomach—each release clamping his insides down on my dick.

Jesse tugged me closer to him with his legs and wrapped his arms around my neck and kissed me—a reminder of our pact with one another.

After my knot subsided, I slipped free of Jesse's ass and dropped onto the bed beside him. In an unusual move for Jesse, he curled up against me with his head on my chest.

I hugged him to me and kissed his head.

"Carter and I were talking," he said.

Oh, finally.

"About what?"

Jesse stayed silent as he brushed his fingers through the abundant hair on my chest.

"How we both want a cub."

I carded my fingers through his hair. We had talked about adopting someday. Maybe Carter and Shaun were thinking the same thing. It was a comforting dream.

"What if ...."

Then he fell quiet again. Whatever he wanted to say, he was having trouble spitting it out.

"Jesse, you can tell me anything. You know that."

He huffed out a deep breath. "What if Carter and I had a cub together?"

I'm sorry ... what?

I tightened my grip on him and furrowed my brow. What the hell was he on about?

"You want to impregnate Carter?"

"I want to have a cub with Carter, for him and Shaun ... and for us. We would share custody. The cub would have four protectors. They would be surrounded by love."

My mind raced as I processed what Jesse was suggesting.

I had more than one concern, but this one stepped forward in my mind.

"You used to be in love with him. Are you sure this is a good idea?"

Jesse lifted his head and looked down at me. "Are you worried that Carter and I will rekindle what we once had? Because that won't happen. Sure, I love him, and that makes this whole idea even better, but as a friend. I don't want to be his mate, and he doesn't want to be mine. We've found love with you and Shaun. Neither one of us wants to leave behind our true loves."

I grunted. I knew our love was strong ... was I feeling jealousy that Jesse could mate with Carter and produce a precious being we couldn't give each other? Maybe I was—

I needed to shut that down.

Jesse and I were forever.

"When would this happen?"

"Maybe in another year. I'm still in the early stages of my recovery, and I want to be healthy and ready before bringing a cub into our lives."

I agreed with him, plus I had a lot to think about.

"It'll take me a while to get used to the idea, but honestly, I wouldn't be able to find another bear shifter as loving and caring as I know Carter would be with a cub. Shaun, too."

Jesse lowered his head and smiled against my shoulder. "It'll be perfect. I know it will."

I cupped his head and hummed against it. "You're beautiful when you're excited about life."

"You've brought me here."

"No, I think we've brought one another. I was lonely and fully expecting to go through life alone until you came along. You invigorated me. Made me view the world differently."

And so much more.

"I love you," I said.

"Love you, too, my Alpha."

Who could have imagined that a lengthy romp in a hotel room would lead to this? I never would have considered Jesse as a potential mate. He was too broken and too lost.

And exactly what I needed.

Marrying Jesse was the best thing that had ever happened to me.

CHAPTER 16

JESSE

The cabin was cold without a fire burning in the fireplace, which I had fed many times while Carter, Rory, and I lived here. There was dust on the few décor pieces Carter had bought.

I dug around in my dresser drawer and withdrew a few pairs of socks that had seen better days. I dumped them all into the black garbage bag in my hand. The closet was next to empty.

I smiled as I perused the slutty outfits that had been my uniform for years. They all ended up in the garbage bag. That life was a distant memory. One I had no intention of revisiting.

I checked the bathroom on the way to the living room. I found a few shampoo bottles and a dried-up soap. Carter and Rory wouldn't mind if I relegated everything to the trash.

Carter was busy emptying the fridge when I entered the main, open space.

I stopped him before he started dumping the condiments.

"You may want to hold off on that," I said.

He put some ketchup back in the door and crossed his arms. "We need to clear this place out so the new tenants can move in. Sandy said they want it by the first of the month."

"That's not a given."

Carter frowned at me. What Carter didn't know was that Charles had called me to his care home last week. When I arrived, he was sitting with a smartly dressed human male.

He'd pushed some paperwork at me when I sat down.

This is what I wanted to do with his gift.

I dug around in my pocket and produced the keys for the front and back doors of the cabin, then grasped Carter's hand, turned it palm up, and placed the keys in it.

"Why are you giving me these?"

"Because this is your home now ... if you want it."

His brow furrowed even further. "What do you mean?"

"Charles gave me the cabin. It's mine." I touched his chest. "Now, it's yours. You can't exactly raise our cub in that tiny apartment of yours and Shaun's."

Carter covered his mouth with his other hand, then created a gap. "Are you serious?"

"This place was your dream, Carter. Now, it's yours. I'll sign it over to you."

"I'll own it ...."

"Your own small piece of the forest."

Carter leapt at me and yanked me into a hug. "Thank you ... thank you." He kissed my cheek then stepped back, grinning. "Shaun is going to be so excited. You have no idea."

It felt good to give him this. I'd loved him once and treated him horribly over the years, but through it all, he'd stuck by me. He was the kind of friend others dreamed of.

After hugging Rory ... he let me do that now, I looked around the living room. Carter's insistence had changed our lives. This place—this cabin had been pivotal in doing the same.

We had arrived here from the brink of ultimately untimely death and found comfort and community. We had discovered peace, and then one by one, we'd found love.

I owed my life to the sequence of events that had brought me here.

One more look at the amber log walls, then I made my way outside. Lucas was standing beside his truck door, waiting for me. He'd left me to go in on my own.

Carter, Rory, and I had needed to do this ourselves.

I slung the garbage bag into the back of his truck and joined him as he climbed into the cab. He'd left the motor running, keeping it warm against the icy winter cold.

I turned in my seat before we got going.

"I gave Carter the keys." I smiled. "He's ecstatic."

Lucas chuckled. "Thought he might be. It's quite the gift."

"He deserves it. Without him, I wouldn't be here with you."

Lucas took my hand. "Then I owe him my life."

I needed to get something out while we were sitting here. So many memories of who I had been before—the drugs and alcohol—the sex work ... it all tumbled forward.

"I want to thank you for fighting for us and not walking away from my chaos. I never could have imagined someone would see worth in me. That I was desirable as a mate even though I was a mess. That you would stand by me. That you would love me and make me yours."

Lucas lifted my hand and kissed my knuckles.

There were no words needed. I could see everything I desired to know in his eyes.

I looked at the cabin that had brought me here, then at Lucas.

"Take me home."

LONE WOLF

URBAN CRIME MM WOLF SHIFTER MPREG ROMANCE

T he love stories continue in Metro City. Mason Black, the second son of Lucas and Adam Black, is all grown up and living in Metro City as a detective for the city's police department.

I never thought my life would turn out like this. I left Creekside Township at the age of sixteen, full of hope, heading to Metro City to pursue my dream of chasing down murderers and thieves.

Instead, my innocence was stolen.

Now, I can't sleep or relax without distractions. My life and desires are messed up.

I'm broken.

I'm a lone wolf that seeks pleasure for pleasure's sake. I'm also the youngest detective the Metro City Police Department has ever promoted to lead a murder investigation.

I prefer to work alone, but the sergeant has other ideas, forcing me to work with a human partner. Even when my new partner sees my dark side, my life in the shadows, he doesn't run.

For the first time in a long time, I feel it ... hope.

Lone Wolf is a spin-off from the Creekside Township Rivals series. One of the main characters, Mason Black, is the grown son of Lucas and Adam Black, the fated mates in Book 1 - *Lucas' Omega*. This story is a mix of **murder mystery** and **wolf shifter MPreg** romance.

Available on Amazon and other retailers.

ABOUT THE AUTHOR

J T Fader is the fantasy and paranormal pen name of queer, bigender author Leigh Jarrett (she/he). Writing MM+ romance with a speculative twist, JT Fader explores magical worlds, supernatural beings, and otherworldly love stories filled with emotion, grit, and passion.

Their work blends the fantastical with deep character connection, featuring queer protagonists on transformative journeys.

Based on Vancouver Island, JT Fader brings the same heart and authenticity found in Leigh Jarrett's contemporary work to realms of magic, myth, and epic fantasy.

To check out more of JT Fader's titles, visit their website.